Sweeping the Crime Under the Rug . . .

Longarm was about to leave when something on the floor caught his eye. It was the rug, and it was pushed up against a wall so that it was slightly bowed. Normally, such a small thing would not have caught his attention, but the rest of the bedroom was so orderly that it seemed odd.

"Hmmm," he mused aloud, staring at the round rug, which was roughly six feet in diameter, and then on impulse tugging at it. It seemed to be cemented to the floor, and he had to put the lantern down and really put his back to it to tear the rug up from the floor. He tossed it aside and then picked up the lantern for a closer look.

"Oh, my," he said, taking in a sharp breath, because under the rug and no doubt causing it to feel pasted to the floor was a very large, crusted, and blackened pool of blood.

"Murder," he said to himself as he found his pocketknife, unfolded the longest blade, and began to scrape at the blood. "Someone was murdered right here in this room . . ."

TABOR EVANS

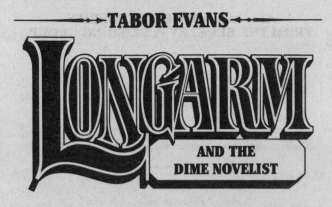

LONGARM

AND THE
DIME NOVELIST

JOVE BOOKS, NEW YORK

THE BERKLEY PUBLISHING GROUP
Published by the Penguin Group
Penguin Group (USA) LLC
375 Hudson Street, New York, New York 10014

USA • Canada • UK • Ireland • Australia • New Zealand • India • South Africa • China

penguin.com

A Penguin Random House Company

LONGARM AND THE DIME NOVELIST

A Jove Book / published by arrangement with the author

For information, address: The Berkley Publishing Group,
a division of Penguin Group (USA) LLC,
375 Hudson Street, New York, New York 10014.

ISBN: 978-0-515-15431-3

PUBLISHING HISTORY
Jove mass-market edition / February 2014

PRINTED IN THE UNITED STATES OF AMERICA

10 9 8 7 6 5 4 3 2 1

Cover illustration by Milo Sinovcic.

Chapter 1

Deputy United States Marshal Custis Long arrived at his office in the Federal Building on a cold, snowy morning on the second day of January. He made his way carefully up the ice-crusted steps and entered the foyer, nodding at a clerk who sat behind a desk checking on the comings and goings of visitors. The man's name was Otis and he was friendly and in his early sixties. Otis had once been a law officer, but he'd caught a bullet in the knee and now he walked with a pronounced limp. Longarm knew that Otis kept a bottle of whiskey in his desk to numb the constant pain he felt from the old wound. To Longarm's way of thinking, Otis had paid his dues and deserved whatever help he needed to get through his often boring workday.

"Morning, Marshal Long. How were your holidays?" Otis asked, glancing over the top of his daily newspaper.

Longarm stomped the snow off his boots and removed his gloves. The temperature outside was bitterly cold and a steady southwesterly wind made it seem even colder. Inside the big Federal Building the temperature was probably only about sixty degrees, but it felt very warm so Long-arm removed his heavy coat.

"Otis, my holidays are always pretty quiet," he told the clerk.

"No family visits?"

"Nope."

"That's right," Otis said, looking a little embarrassed. "I forgot that you told me you were a confirmed bachelor. You know, Marshal, you ought to find a good woman and make her honest. I was single like you for a lot of years when I was in law enforcement. Then, after I was shot and had to take this desk job, I met my wife, Anna. I've been a far happier man while married than when I was single. You really ought to think about taking a wife."

"Yeah." Longarm unbuttoned his coat and slapped some snow off his flat-brimmed, snuff-brown hat. He had heard this same advice from the old lawman at least a hundred times already. "You're probably right."

"Of course I am! And with your reputation as a ladies' man, you could have your pick of about any woman you set your eyes upon. In fact, I know of two good single women who work in this building that would love to get to know you better."

"That right?"

"Sure is! You want to know who they are?"

"Nope."

Otis didn't even attempt to hide his disappointment. "Well, like I said, getting shot in the knee changed my whole life for the better."

"Glad you feel that way, Otis." Longarm liked and respected the man but sometimes found Otis a little bit pushy when offering his opinions.

"I tell you this," Otis said as Longarm headed across the marble foyer toward the stairwell leading up to his second floor office, "the holidays can be mighty lonesome and sad without a wife and family. I got two lovely daughters and they're the reason that me and Anna put up a Christmas tree and make such a big deal of the holidays. Without a wife and kids, a man is bound to be miserable this time of the year."

"I'll survive," Longarm called over his shoulder as he entered the stairwell. "But thanks for your concern."

"You really ought to let me tell you about those two women that are after your body!" Otis shouted. "They're awful good-lookin'!"

Longarm grinned and took the stairs two at a time. When he entered the office where he and his fellow workers spent their workday, he waved at a few of the other deputy marshals, tossed his coat, hat, and gloves on his desk, and headed for the little room where there was always hot coffee brewing.

"Hey," a marshal named Pete Schilling said, raising his own cup of coffee. "How was your holiday?"

"Pretty quiet."

"Well, that's because you insist on remaining a bachelor and playing the field instead of finding a good woman to marry like my Clara."

"Yeah," Longarm said, trying to curb his mounting irritation, "we all reap what we sow, eh?"

"You could put it that way, I suppose."

Longarm wasn't going to hurt the man's feelings by pointing out that Pete's wife was as fat as a sow and about as pretty as the butt end of a boar hog. No sir, he was just going to endure everyone telling him he ought to put himself in bondage and become a henpecked husband. Why the hell was it that married men seemed so determined that all their single friends follow their lead into marital bondage?

"Say," the deputy said, turning around in the doorway. "The boss has a visitor who is asking about you. He's been pacing around waiting for you to finally come in this morning."

"Billy needs to see me about a visitor?"

"That's right. And she's a beauty. You didn't go and leave her in a bad fix, did you?"

Longarm scowled even though he was almost legendary as a ladies' man and much more than commonly promiscuous. "Look, Pete, I haven't even had my first cup of coffee and you know I'm not one to talk about the ladies I date, so why don't you just put a cork in your ass before I start to put this coffee cup in it instead?"

Pete was about as thick-skinned and intelligent as an alligator. He wasn't listening and laughed. "You call taking your women to bed having a 'date'?"

"Pete, I'm warning you to lay off. I'm not in a mood to be trifled with this morning."

"Yeah, you look wrung out all right. You know what? I've always been amazed that you haven't been taken to court by a dozen or so women you got pregnant. Why, I'll bet you have at least four or five bastards running around loose in Denver."

Longarm had heard more than enough and he wasn't one to warn a man twice. Pete was obnoxious and he liked to goad people into getting angry before he backed off and tried to make a joke of his behavior. But not this morning. Pete needed to be taught a lesson, so Longarm slapped Pete's steamy cup of coffee splashing it across his shirt and face.

"Owww!" Pete howled, almost tripping as he backed up fast, wiping the coffee from his face. "Damnit, Custis, you had no call to do that!"

"Sure I did," Longarm growled. "And the next time you try to put a burr under my saddle blanket I'm going to rearrange your face so that you'll be even uglier than your fat wife. How does that sound?"

Pete shook his head and reached for his handkerchief. "The thing I don't understand is how you have lived as long as you have given your shitty attitude and quick temper."

Longarm moved toward Pete with his fist balled, but the man was smart enough to backpedal around a desk, then turn and scurry off.

"Asshole," Longarm muttered, going back into the coffee room and taking his cup off a hook then filling it. He didn't use sugar or cream because, to his way of thinking, if a fella had to doctor up the taste of his coffee, then he might just as well not have any.

"Happy holidays," a voice said behind him. "I see that you're in your usual sour postholiday mood."

Longarm turned to see his boss, Marshal Billy Vail. Vail was of average height compared to Longarm's six feet four inches and physically unimposing, but he was one of the best lawmen in the building and a fine boss to work for . . . if you had to work for anyone at all.

"Aw," Longarm said, "it was Pete trying to get my goat. I just lost my patience with him and then he accidentally splashed coffee all over himself."

"Yeah," Billy said, "I'm sure it was an accident. Custis, you shouldn't let jerks like that get under your skin."

"And you need to fire him," Longarm countered. "But until you do I'll try to take that advice to heart. Otis said that someone was asking for me first thing this morning."

"That's right. Did Otis also happen to mention that it is a woman and a very pretty one at that?"

"He did. Otis is always trying to get me paired up with some woman who is looking for a husband. Is that what this is about?"

"No," Billy said. "This woman is definitely not looking for a husband unless maybe he's rich, which you definitely are not."

"Glad to hear that." Longarm took a sip of coffee and as usual found it to be weak. "You need to spend a little more money on the coffee fund, Billy. This stuff is as weak as tea."

"It's paid for with taxpayer money so you shouldn't be bitching. Go ahead, swill it down and let's go see what this woman wants with you. She claims to be Governor Grover Wilson's daughter and . . . if that's true . . . you need to be polite and respectful."

Longarm mentally ran through some pretty faces that he'd dated and bedded, but he was sure that none of them had claimed to be the governor's daughter. "I'm always respectful to a lady, Billy. Southern upbringing. But in all honesty, I can't imagine why such a woman would want to see me."

"I can't, either," Billy agreed. "But she did ask me an odd question."

"And that was?"

"Her name is Delia and she asked me if you were literate."

Longarm almost choked on his coffee. "What!"

"You heard me." Billy was trying his best not to smile. "And while I assured her that you were not a man to be found in a library, I told her that you were indeed literate and considerably smarter than you looked."

"Thanks a million."

"You're welcome," Billy said, ignoring the sarcasm. "But here's the interesting thing. Delia then asked me if you liked to read dime novels."

"Dime novels?"

"That's what she asked."

Longarm scowled. "What kind of a silly question is *that*?"

"Beats me. I tried to press her for some answers regarding her interest in meeting you, but she deftly sidestepped everything and mentioned that she'd heard a lot about you and wanted to make your acquaintance."

"Fine," Longarm said, starting to get real curious. "Is she *really* a looker . . . or are you just setting me up for a fright? I wouldn't put it past any of you."

"Delia is gorgeous," Billy said, throwing up his hands. "Long blond hair, blue eyes, a figure that would make any man drool over, and lips that . . . well, let's just say that she ought to be outlawed around a bachelor as randy as yourself."

"If she's that attractive and the daughter of our governor, then I'm sure she is completely out of my class and knows how to handle far more successful men very well."

"We'll see." Billy gestured toward the cup of coffee in Longarm's hand. "Why don't you leave that here for later and come meet Miss Delia Wilson? I'm as curious as you are as to why she wants to know if you read dime novels."

"Just for your information, I never read them. They're pretty much bullshit."

"I know, but extremely popular."

Longarm shrugged his broad shoulders. "They're still bullshit."

"Custis, please refrain from saying that to the young lady. Just be the southern gentleman that you were taught to be where you learned your manners back in West Virginia. And I know that you can layer the charm on with the best of them, Custis. Wouldn't hurt to do that this morning because I don't want Delia to go back to her father with bad things to say about the treatment she received at our office."

"The last time I checked you didn't work for or take your orders from Governor Wilson."

"That's true," Billy agreed, "I don't. But you never know what will come down the pike, and in my job it always pays to make friends and avoid making enemies . . . especially among the politically powerful." Billy clapped Longarm on the shoulder. "Just be your most charming self and let's find out what is on the young woman's mind."

"Fair enough," Longarm agreed. "But I don't care how important or pretty she is, I'm not kissing her butt or doing something unbecoming to my office."

"Oh, horseshit," Billy muttered as he turned to leave with a smile of amusement. "I got a feeling that kissing her lovely butt wouldn't be that unpleasant."

Longarm burst out laughing. "Wait until the next time you have me over for supper and I tell your sweet wife what you just said!"

"Do that and I'll poison your damned coffee and after you are buried I'll piss all over your grave," Billy called back.

Longarm gulped down the rest of his coffee. First Otis downstairs had badgered him about marriage, then Pete about maybe having some illegitimate children running around town, and now his boss and best friend Billy Vail threatening him with poisoned coffee.

This first day after the holidays was quickly going to hell in a handbasket, and he had a feeling things weren't going to get any better after he found out why in the world the governor's daughter wanted to know if he ever read those wildly popular but incredibly ridiculous dime novels with titles like *Bloody Day at Black Rock*, *Guts and Six-guns*, or *The Badmen and the Even Worse Bad Women*.

Once, his barber had told him the plot of a popular dime novel and it had concerned a gunfighter who had gotten three of his fingers shot off so he had learned to throw hatchets with amazing speed and accuracy. And so this two-fingered ex-gunfighter had gone around throwing hatchets left and right and sometimes, just to warn his opponent, he'd throw the hatchets so accurately he sliced off ears!

Ridiculous!

Longarm was shaking his head when he turned a corner in the office and saw Delia sitting in front of Billy's desk. She was so good-looking he stopped in his tracks and let out a low whistle before he smoothed down his long, curly hair. Well, well, he thought, swallowing hard, maybe this first day back after the holidays was going to be more enjoyable than he'd expected!

Chapter 2

"Miss Wilson," Billy said, "this is my finest deputy marshal, Custis Long, better known as Longarm."

Delia looked Custis up and down, then smiled and extended her hand. "I've heard so very much about you and at last we meet."

"So we do," Longarm said. "How is the governor these days?"

"My father is doing just fine except that he slipped on some ice and took a hard fall outside the capitol building. We were afraid he'd broken his arm, but that wasn't the case and he's mending. He just hates this snow and cold weather."

"Well," Longarm said, "we do get plenty of that in Denver and this winter seems to have been worse than usual."

"I agree. We have at least two feet of snow on the ground, and I'm sure we'll get another storm before the week passes." Delia glanced at a chair. "Marshal Long, I'd like to talk to you for a few minutes about my next dime novel."

Longarm shrugged. "You mean that you've written several?"

"Thirty-six to be exact. Of course, I don't write under my own name. I use the pen name of Dakota Walker."

"Nice," Longarm said, trying to seem impressed.

"I'd use my own name, of course, but the readers of dime novels are mostly men and they don't think that a woman could possibly write scenes of real violence and bloodshed."

"Do you sell many?"

"Oh, yes, my latest novel, *Blood on the Bar Room Floor*, has already sold over eight thousand copies and it's only been on the shelves for a month. Before it sells out it should top ten thousand and I get three cents a copy, so you can see that it will make me three hundred dollars."

"Well, how about that," Longarm said.

"I write them in about a week."

"That is amazing."

She shrugged. "Not really. They aren't long and I have a very *vivid and bawdy* imagination. Most men like a little titillation mixed with their violence . . . or at least that's my experience."

Longarm saw a smile form at the corners of her mouth and her blue eyes dropped below his belt. He swallowed hard and managed to keep his mind on what direction this conversation was taking.

Billy's face had actually turned red with embarrassment and he quickly said, "Why don't I leave you two here to talk in private for a few minutes? I've got some things that need attending to out in the office."

"That would be fine," Delia said sweetly. "And I want to thank you for being so generous with your time this morning. I promise that I won't keep your famous deputy marshal for long."

"Take as much time as you need," Billy said, heading for the door.

When they were alone, Longarm gestured for Delia to

take a seat and he did the same. "We've got coffee brewing, but it's lousy."

"Thanks, but no, thanks." She was wearing a beautiful coral-colored dress and now she lifted her right leg and rested it on her knee revealing a lovely curve of ankle. "I suppose you're wondering why I wanted to meet you this morning."

"Well, yes, I am."

Delia sighed and for a moment, looked sad. "The truth is that I've milked the cow dry."

"The what?"

"It's a literary term meaning I've run out of story ideas."

"I see."

"Thirty-six dime novels have made me quite a lot of money. My New York publishers want me to write one a month."

"If they earn you three hundred dollars each, that's a lot of money every year," Longarm mused, genuinely impressed as he totaled the figures in his mind.

"Yes, it's more than my father makes as governor. But, like I said, I've about milked the cow of imagination dry." She waited for Longarm to say something and when he didn't, she added, "And that's why I need your help."

"I don't understand."

"I need fresh fodder for the cow so she'll produce new, exciting stories for my growing legion of fans."

"And you think I can provide the . . . the fodder?"

"I sure do. I've heard about you for years. I know that you've shot and killed dozens of men in the line of duty and that you've been shot, stabbed, and beaten. I'm sure that you have the scars to prove how much danger you have faced in this job."

"I've killed plenty of men, but that's not something I'm especially proud of."

"Really?"

"Yes, really."

"I'm glad to hear that. So, no guilt at all?"

"There were a few that were drunk and I wished I could have pistol-whipped instead of shot," Longarm hedged.

"Have you ever had to shoot a woman?"

"Yes."

"Does that bother you more than the men you've killed?"

"Miss Wilson, is there a point to these questions?" Longarm asked.

"I'm just trying to understand."

"Then I'll say this much. I don't like to kill . . . and I've taken an oath to protect. But there have been a few men that I was actually proud to eliminate. Men who were purely evil and would have continued to prey on others by killing and robbing them."

"I'm glad to hear you say that. I recall you were the one that finally caught Bad John Bixby, the infamous murderer and rapist. I understand that you cornered him and shoved your revolver up his ass when he was humping a fifteen-year-old girl and blew his balls off."

Longarm's jaw dropped. "That's not true!"

"Then what really happened?"

Longarm shook his head. "Are you sure you want to hear the details? It wasn't pretty."

"Rape and murder never are. And yes, I really want to hear the details . . . all of them exactly as it happened."

"If I tell you the details, you'd use my name and that wouldn't be good for either me . . . or this department."

"You had to file a formal report and I'm sure that when you were called to court to testify to the killing before a judge you had to give him the details under oath."

"Yes, I did."

"So the details are public record."

"No," Longarm said, correcting her. "When we file a report of a shooting . . . especially one that results in death . . . that report remains strictly confidential. And when I go before a judge, which isn't often, what I say about a killing is taken under oath but kept out of the public record. The judge has to hear the true facts and he decides if the killing was justified."

"I understand," Delia said, "otherwise you or your department could be sued or charged with murder. The confidentiality is to protect you while you are performing your sworn duty to uphold the law and track down outlaws and murderers."

"That's right."

Delia pulled pencil and pad out of her coat pocket and pursed her lips in thought for a moment before speaking. "What if we do a . . . *suppose*?"

"What do you mean by that?"

"Well, you could use suppose you did this and suppose you did that never actually admitting that you did anything."

"Sounds complicated, Miss Wilson."

"It isn't really. Let me give you a brief example. You could say you *suppose* that you might have talked to a man in a saloon who knew someone that had bragged about all the women he had raped and then stabbed to death. And then you spent some time hanging out in that saloon and when the braggart finally appeared a week later, the man who had tipped you off gave you a signal so that you knew this was the rapist and killer. And then you suppose you could have tracked him to his house and watched him for a day or two and he slipped away but you saw and followed him down a dark street in a poor part of this town and when you saw him strip down naked and enter a girl's bedroom window. You knew what was going to happen and burst through the front door, gun in hand and caught the man already on top of the screaming girl. You were so outraged that you could have rammed the barrel of your pistol up his ass and pulled the trigger five times."

"If I'd have done that, my bullets might have gone through his body and into the girl's body."

"That's right," Delia said, "but you might have first yanked him off the victim and then slung him to the floor before the bullets made a big mess of what had been his—"

"Hold it up there!" Longarm snapped, interrupting Delia. "This is getting way too ugly for me to talk about."

Delia closed her pretty mouth and then she put her pencil and pad away. "What if I told you that I know that is pretty close to what happened in that girl's bedroom the night that you killed Bad John Bixby?"

Longarm came to his feet. "And how would you know those kinds of details?"

Delia smiled sweetly. "I have access to inside information."

Longarm had heard enough. When he'd emptied his gun into the ass of the rapist and murderer, he'd been so enraged that he'd momentarily lost control and taken his bloody vengeance. And in his office report and sworn and secret testimony before a judge, he'd admitted to the shooting, saying that the room was dark and he'd had to act swiftly in order to save not only the girl's life but his own. The fact that his bullets had all entered the rapist's ass had simply been coincidental and hastily done in the line of duty. And besides, he hadn't actually shoved the barrel of his gun up the killer's ass, he'd just pointed it in that direction before he started shooting.

"Marshal?" Delia asked, raising her eyebrows in question. "Have I offended or upset you?"

"No."

"Then why are you looking at me that way?"

"What way?"

"As if I'm a monster or ghoul."

Longarm sat back down. "Are you trying to blackmail me into telling you details about the things that sometimes have to be done in order for a lawman to do his job under gunfire?"

"Not at all! I'm just asking you to tell me stories."

"About?"

"What you supposedly could have done in certain situations when you have been fighting for your life or fighting to save someone else's life . . . like the life of that fifteen-year-old girl."

"And what if I say that I'd rather not have anything to do with what you are proposing . . . even if it is *supposing*?"

Delia came to her feet. "Marshal Long, I have read everything I could find about you and you are undoubtedly the most honorable, brave, and capable lawman I've ever heard of or are likely to meet. I know for a fact that you have killed no less than twenty-four men and that every one of them deserved to die hard. I wouldn't dream of using your name or sullying your reputation. I just need fodder for my imagination so that the milk of creativity begins to flow once more."

"I'm not going to do it," Longarm said, turning toward the door. "I think this conversation is over."

"Not by a mile."

He turned back to her. "What does that mean, Miss Wilson?"

"It means that I insist on your cooperation and if it is not freely given, I can make things very bad for you."

"You'd do that?"

"Only if I have to." She stepped close. "Don't make me have to do anything that would harm you or your boss."

"I don't like being threatened. And I don't care if you are the daughter of our governor."

"How much money do you make a month?"

"Enough."

"You can never have enough money. I will pay you well and give you my word that no one will ever have any idea of what you supposed regarding some of your most exciting and bloody episodes."

Longarm took her arm and squeezed it just hard enough to make her wince. "Miss Wilson," he said, physically shoving her toward the door. "We're done talking."

"I need your help."

"Help I'm not willing to give."

"I want to meet you for dinner, buy you a steak and some expensive wine, and then take you to my home and give you dessert."

There was no mistaking her intentions, but even so Longarm was shocked by her frankness. "And I would enjoy this 'dessert' at the governor's mansion?"

"No, I own my own home. I'm a big girl now in case you haven't noticed."

Longarm pushed her out the door. "I'm sorry but I've already got plans for this evening."

"Break them! I promise that you won't be sorry."

"Miss Wilson, after this conversation I already am sorry," he told her as he shut the door in her lovely face.

"What happened?" Billy Vail asked when he reentered his office and saw Longarm sitting in a chair with a thoughtful look on his face.

"She is unlike anyone I've ever met before," Longarm replied.

"In a good way . . . or a bad one?"

"Depends on your point of view."

"Well, what did she want?"

Longarm stood up. "She wants stories from me about what I've done . . . especially the most violent stories. She wants the details about who I've killed in the line of duty so that she can change the names and write more of her dime novels."

"Hmmm," Billy mused. "I think you'd be treading on thin legal ice if you cooperated with Miss Wilson."

"I know that." Longarm shook his head. "The thing of it is, Billy, she's trying to force my hand into this arrangement whether I like it or not."

"I see." Billy walked around his desk and had a seat. "Being as she is our governor's daughter, this could get complicated."

"More than you can imagine," Longarm agreed. "What do you think that I should do?"

"Frankly, I'm not sure. I've never had one of my marshals come face-to-face with this kind of thing. Did the woman actually threaten you?"

"It was the old carrot or stick kind of approach," Longarm explained. "She promised to pay me well and that she'd never divulge my name and keep my identity secret."

"That might be acceptable."

"But when I refused," Longarm said, "she told me that she could damage my reputation and that of this department by getting access to information and reports that are supposed to be kept secret."

"Then she really is dangerous."

"Oh," Longarm said, "she's that all right. She might just be the most cunning and dangerous woman I've ever met."

"You should just avoid her."

"I'm going to try to do that, Billy. But I have this feeling that Miss Delia Wilson, aka dime novelist Dakota Walker, will not allow herself to be shunned or avoided."

"We have an attorney at our disposal, Custis. Maybe you should have a discussion with him and find out what he'd advise."

"That might be good advice, Billy. But I think I need to know a little more about Miss Wilson before I go to see a lawyer. She invited me to dinner, but I declined saying I already had plans."

"Do you?"

"Yes, but they can be changed and I've no doubt that Delia is not the kind to take no for an answer concerning tonight."

"You can't go to our governor if she tries to twist your arm. If you did that, he'd be offended and nothing good would come of it."

"I know that."

"Then how . . ."

"She invited me to dinner tonight and then to have some dessert."

"Well, a good steak and a slice of cherry or apple pie would be nice, I suppose."

It was all that Longarm could do not to laugh out loud. Billy, bless his good and honest heart, really was a child when it came to understanding wild and wicked women.

Chapter 3

Longarm left his quarters at about eight o'clock that evening wearing a fresh shirt and shave. He paused under the lights outside and selected a cigar from his coat pocket, then lit it and began to carefully move down the icy sidewalk. He was headed for the nearby Timberline Steak House, and he wondered if Delia was watching and waiting somewhere to intercept him.

Longarm was not sure he wanted to be intercepted by the lovely dime novelist. Yes, he was definitely attracted to her physically and it would be interesting and highly pleasurable to make love to her . . . but he knew that pleasure would come at a very steep price. It was almost a certainty that Delia would expect him to succumb to her considerable charms and become compliant and agreeable to her requests for detailed recounts of his adventures and deadly shoot-outs. In some ways, that might be fun, and as long as his true identity remained secret Longarm could not foresee a problem. But if Delia broke her promise not to use his name, then he would be helpless to stop the considerable damage that would befall his reputation and that of his department.

Longarm supposed that the basic question was . . . if he climbed into her bed and her world, could he control her? And the answer, he reluctantly concluded was that he probably could not.

A buggy pulled by two fine horses rolled past and the driver waved at Longarm, who stood waiting on the corner. It was so cold out that the ice crackled under the wheels and steam shot out of the nostrils of the matched team as if they were a pair of small, black dragons in harness.

"Evening!" the man called to Longarm who was the only one out on the sidewalk.

"Evening," Longarm shouted in reply. He crossed the dimly lit street and then started up the sidewalk when a voice called to him. "Custis!"

Longarm knew before turning around that it was Delia.

"So," Delia said, stepping out of a millinery shop and slipping her arm through his own, "Could this lonesome girl buy you that steak dinner and dessert that she promised?"

Longarm tried to say no. But looking into her lovely face with her cheeks rosy from the cold and her blue eyes sparkling, he found he could not say a word. Her expensive perfume clouded the cold air and it was easy to imagine how wonderful her luscious, warm body would feel pressed up against his own later on this bitterly cold night. Not surprisingly, he found himself nodding his head.

"You have someplace to eat in mind?"

"King's Steak House. Have you been there before?"

"No," he admitted, "it's way out of my price range."

"Nothing to worry about tonight, Custis." She squeezed his arm tightly. "This is all free and on me."

They began to walk, shoes crunching the snow, the faint sound of a sleigh bell ringing in the distance. "Delia, somehow I think that even if you pay for the finest meal in Denver, this is still going to cost me plenty."

She looked up at him. "Why don't you trust me just a little and take a chance? We'll talk about this over dinner. I believe I can persuade you that helping me is going to be in both our interests."

"We'll see."

King's Steak House was where the Denver people with money and influence went to eat, and Longarm wondered if his appearance with the governor's stunningly beautiful daughter would turn heads. Because he was quite tall and broad shouldered, he was accustomed to attracting attention, yet tonight it would be for a very different reason.

"Good evening, Miss Wilson!" the maître d' said when they entered the restaurant with its impressive crystal chandeliers, beautiful oil paintings, and even a bubbling marble fountain with fish swimming lazily around in circles. "How nice to see you tonight."

"Thank you, Pierre. Could we have a booth that is quiet and will allow us some privacy?"

"Of course!" Pierre's hawkish eyes skipped over Longarm in the briefest of glances but it was clear that he was unimpressed with the wardrobe her guest was wearing. "Please follow me."

Being that it was a weeknight and so cold outside, there weren't a lot of patrons, but those that were eating stopped and stared as Longarm and Delia were led to a corner booth lit with three candles resting in an ornate silver candelabra.

"I hope this is acceptable," Pierre said to Delia.

"It's perfect. Thank you."

"Can I order you something special to drink before your meal?"

Delia looked to Longarm, who had just removed his coat and handed it to the man. "Custis? A good French wine?"

"A double shot of your best whiskey for starters," he said, thinking that what the hell, if he was going to be feted, then he was going to have it done to his liking instead of Delia's or what the uppity Pierre thought was sophisticated or proper.

"Yes, sir! That would be Kentucky Gold, aged ten years and as smooth as silk on the palate but with an ever-so-slight and delicious taste of oak."

"Sounds good to me," Longarm said, turning to Delia. "And what are you having?"

"Well, maybe I'll have the same," Delia said, looking as if she were trying to match Custis in some sort of contest of wills.

Pierre gave Delia a very slight look of disapproval, but he was smiling all the while and bowed. "As you wish. Be right back with your drinks."

"So," Longarm said, once they were alone, "you're a whiskey drinker?"

"Not normally." She brightened. "Can I recommend the veal with cherry sauce? It is my favorite and I'm sure you won't be disappointed."

Longarm inspected the menu and was instantly glad that he was not paying the tab. The prices were outrageous. The wine list started at fifteen dollars a bottle and went up to seventy-five with the average price being fifty dollars. All the wines were French, mostly cabernet and merlot . . . they were rich, dark wines that he favored on the rare occasions when he did drink good wine.

They ordered and chatted about small things while they sipped whiskey. "What do you think?" she asked.

"About the whiskey?"

She waved her hand overhead in a quick circle. "About *all* of this."

He smacked his lips. "This whiskey is as smooth as it gets. I was born and raised in West Virginia and we had some good moonshine there, but this is on an entirely different level. If the veal is even half as satisfying, I'll be a very happy man tonight."

"Just save something for dessert at my place," she said quietly as her hand slipped under the table and came to rest on his thigh.

My oh my, Longarm thought, *this might be the dumbest thing I've done in a long time but I'm sure going to have fun at it.*

Two hours later, they stepped back outside into the cold feeling tipsy and merry. The air was so cold it took their breath away, but Longarm managed to say, "Delia, thank you for the unbelievable meal and the drinks. The wine was especially nice . . . but I'm not sure we should have ordered that second bottle."

"It's only money and besides, I get a large discount."

"You do?"

"Sure. When my father comes here with important people, they tend to spend a lot of money and they tip the help generously. So in return, I do receive a substantial discount."

"I had no idea that was how it worked."

"It works that way when people have mutual goals that equally benefits both parties."

"Like I've just benefitted?"

"That's right. I've made no secret that I am happy to provide you things that you might not ordinarily be able to afford and to pay you well for your help . . . but that I expect you to help me. How more honest could I possibly be?"

"You've been quite honest," Longarm admitted. "But . . ."

"But what?" she asked as they walked slowly down the slippery sidewalk. "What is your biggest concern?"

"That you'll go back on your word and use my name in your stories."

She shook her head. "Custis, I've told you that I don't even use my own name. Remember? I'm Dakota Walker."

"True." They had both had enough to drink so that they were immune to the severe cold, but Longarm knew that would soon wear off. "Do you live far from here?"

"No. We're almost there."

"Good."

"Yes," she agreed. "I think we're both ready for warmth and dessert."

"You're reading my mind, Miss Wilson."

"Delia . . . or Dakota, please."

"Delia," he said as they turned up a walk toward a small mansion. Longarm stopped and studied the home. "Do you own this and live here all by yourself?"

"Yes, but even writing a dime novel a month doesn't buy this kind of a house in this kind of a neighborhood."

"And you said you made more money than your father does as governor."

"The money that bought this house and so many other things . . . since you're obviously curious . . . comes from Philadelphia. You see, my mother inherited a fortune from my grandfather, who owned a railroad."

"Didn't your mother pass away a few years ago?" Longarm asked as they neared the door.

"That's right. She committed suicide."

Longarm was suddenly sober. "I'm sorry."

"It was her choice," Delia said, fitting a key into the door. "My father was cheating on her . . . he always cheated on my mother . . . and she drank heavily to drown her disappointment. And when the liquor wasn't enough and the pain was too great, she took her own life."

"I didn't know that."

"My father made sure that the newspapers said that my mother didn't die of a broken heart or of too much liquor but instead of a sudden coronary failure."

Longarm didn't know what to say so he said nothing as they entered the home and Delia showed him some of the rooms before she led him to the bedroom.

"Custis?"

"Yeah."

"What I told you about my mother is known only by a very few people."

"I understand. I won't say anything."

"I know that because I *trust* you," Delia replied. "And having given you my trust of a very personal nature, I expect the same from you."

Longarm understood, and as he began to undress he decided that he was going to have his dessert and enjoy it, and he remembered an old adage . . . in for a penny, in for a pound. Well, by gawd, he was in for more than a pound and heaven help him if he was setting himself up for being the biggest fool in Colorado.

Chapter 4

"What is that crazy contraption hanging from your bedroom ceiling?" Longarm asked as he undressed.

"There is nothing crazy about it," Delia replied. "And before this night is over, you will think it is a fantastic invention."

"Oh, yeah?"

"Yeah." She kissed him. "Custis, I told you that I'm a very creative person. I designed that myself."

"It looks like a child's swing with stirrups." Longarm finished undressing and went over to look at the thing. "How's it work?"

"You're about to find out," Delia said. "But first, let's get better acquainted in bed."

He turned away from the swing and took in a sharp breath. "My gawd, Delia, your body is a work of art."

She stood naked before him, a slight smile on her moist lips. "You're not so bad as a sculpture yourself, but my oh my, you sure bear the scars of your profession. What happened here?" she asked, touching a long scar across his chest.

"A knife wound. I cornered a half-breed down in El Paso. He had the fastest hands I ever saw on a man."

Delia kissed the scar, her hand dropping to cup his testicles. "Tell me more, big boy."

"Not much to say," Longarm replied, feeling his manhood stiffening. "I went for my gun and he went for his knife and he was obviously a bit faster. After he slashed me across the chest, I grabbed his wrist, broke it and turned the blade around. He took the whole seven inches of that bowie knife in the belly."

She nibbled on his nipples and started working his rod as she whispered, "I'll take *your* whole seven inches. Is it that long, Custis?"

"I never let a woman measure it," he replied, pushing her down on the bed and kissing her lips. "But when we're done, you can if you want."

"Might be longer," she breathed, between kisses.

Longarm kissed her large breasts, then ran his hand up and down her smooth thighs. "You've got beautiful legs."

"That want to crush you between them," she panted.

Longarm mounted Delia, driving his rod deep into her honey pot. "Does it feel like seven . . . or eight?"

"Oh, my!" she gasped. "It feels like a ten-pound sausage!"

He laughed out loud and began to move around in her. Delia wrapped her long legs around his waist and whispered, "Slowly, Custis, very slowly. We've got all night."

He took his time and when they were both breathing hard, he stopped still resting deep inside of her.

"What?" she asked. "I said, slow, not stop."

"I need to see how that contraption hanging from the ceiling works."

"Now?"

"Sure."

"Can't it . . ."

"No, it can't wait."

"All right. Get off of me and I'll show you."

Longarm climbed off the bed. He was long and stiff and slick with her love juices. Delia's eyes were glazed with passion and she jumped off the bed and hurried over to the seat, plopping her beautiful bottom in a swing chair and then lifting her legs and quickly adjusting some straps, and using a little pulley device that actually lifted her body several inches higher. And finally, she planted her heels into the leather stirrups.

"I had to crank this seat higher because you're so damn tall."

He stared at the sight of her wide open with her lovely, long legs stretched far apart. "Quite a sight, Delia, but I'm not sure about this."

"See these chair arms?" she asked, patting them.

"Yeah."

"Well, grab them and you can push and pull yourself in and out of me."

"I was doing that on your bed."

"This will be completely different."

"I doubt that."

"Come on," she pleaded, rubbing herself and wiggling with anticipation. "Back inside me where you belong."

Longarm lined himself up and slipped into her hot wetness. He grasped the arms of the chair swing and started rocking Delia back and forth.

"Huh!" he grunted with a big smile of pleasure on his face. "This is a new one on me."

"Rock me faster. Harder, too!"

Longarm was more than happy to oblige. He began to push and pull the swing energetically. Delia yelped and Longarm quickly got into the spirit of the union. In two or three minutes, he was slamming himself in and out of Delia and his knees were knocking and his butt was pounding. Her head was thrown back, long blond hair swinging from side to side, mouth forming an oval as she groaned and made fierce animal sounds in her throat.

"Good, huh," she managed to grunt, kissing his lips.

"Better than good!"

And so they went at it on the chair swing until Delia cried out, her entire body shaking violently. Longarm was wild with desire and he kept pushing and pulling, ramming and slamming, until his legs felt weak and he'd emptied every last drop of his seed.

When he started to exit her body, she whispered, "Just keep rockin' me, honey. Slower and slower until the feeling is all gone."

"I'm not sure I can stand erect much longer," he said, only half in jest as he clung to the contraption and then finally extracted his tool and staggered over to collapse on the bed.

Delia dropped her feet from the stirrups and using her bare toes rocked herself back and forth, one hand caressing herself as she milked the last bit of pleasure from their union.

"So, Custis," she said lazily as she turned to look at him. "What do you really think?"

"I think you ought to stop writing dime novels and go into business manufacturing those contraptions."

"Really?"

"I'm serious. You could make a fortune."

"Oh, someone in China or someplace where they consider lovemaking an art probably invented something very much like this centuries ago. I read that the Chinese have documented eighty-six unique positions for a man and a woman to couple. I've seen most of them with graphic pictures in books."

"No! Eighty-six?

"Yes."

"Well, if a man and woman tried to do it all those ways they no doubt died of pleasure."

"Not a bad way to go," Delia said with a laugh before she climbed out of the chair swing and came to lie by his side. "I'm so glad you liked my design."

"That would be a huge understatement." Longarm glanced over his shoulders. "The wonder is that we didn't tear the bolts out of the ceiling and crash to the floor."

"Those bolts are six inches long; just a bit shorter than what you screwed me with."

"If you don't mind and you haven't patented the thing, I may make one and put it into my bedroom."

"Why bother when we have this one we can use anytime?"

Longarm grinned. "Yeah, why bother?"

"I need to have a glass of milk," Delia said, rising from the bed. "Or maybe I'll brew a cup of good, hot coffee."

Longarm stood up and consulted his pocket watch. "It's eleven thirty. Perhaps I ought to go back home and get some sleep."

"That's up to you," Delia told him. "I don't have to get up early, but I suppose that you have to be at the office by a certain time."

"I don't," Longarm told her. "Billy expects me in around nine o'clock, but if I'm late he doesn't usually care. He knows that I don't like to sit around waiting for something to happen at the office. I like to be out and about, doing something important, and I hate paperwork."

"I'm sure you do." Delia found a bathrobe and went into the kitchen. "Are you staying or leaving? I'm making the coffee and need to know."

"I'll stick around for a while," Longarm decided, staring at the curve of her hips and breasts pushed up against the fabric of her silk gown. He pulled on his pants and shirt,

then went out into her living room and made his way into
her study and library. There, he looked over a stack of dime
novels, some written under her pseudonym, Dakota Walker,
and at least twenty others written by the most popular dime
novelist of them all, Erastus Flavel Beadle. Longarm knew
that Beadle's Deadwood Dick series had made the author . . .
who had never even come to the West . . . fame and fortune.
The main character in the series, Deadwood Dick, was an
outlaw who had been grievously wronged by powerful, cor-
rupt and wealthy men supported by the law. In dime novel
after dime novel Deadwood Dick always fought for justice
even if he was a wanted man and he was admired for his
generosity and for helping poor ladies in distress. He was a
frontier Robin Hood, a man of great intellect and courage.
Longarm remembered hearing that these dime novels were
particularly popular in the East where people had romantic
illusions about western heroes.

Other novels that Longarm picked up and looked at
included plenty of stories about early frontiersmen who
could shoot with deadly accuracy and cool courage. There
were pictures of men in buckskins fighting bravely against
hordes of Indians intent on lifting their scalps and of ladies
with the bodices of their dresses torn open to reveal ala-
baster white breasts. Most of these women were posed
cringing at the feet of some dime novel hero determined
to save her honor and virginity from terrible, slavering,
and bearded Apaches, outlaws, and even seafaring pirates.

"What a crock of bullshit," Longarm muttered, dropping the books back down on the table with contempt.

"What did you say?" Delia asked, joining him in her
study.

"I have to be honest with you," Longarm told her. "I've
tried to read a few of those dime novels and I either wind

up laughing my butt off . . . or tossing them across the room in disgust."

"Have you ever read one of mine?"

"No. And I hope you aren't offended, but I don't think I ever will."

"I'm not offended. And you are right . . . most dime novels are ridiculous and completely without literary merit. But what I want to write is very different and far more true to life out in the great American West."

"Yeah, you told me you wanted to base your stories on facts."

"And that's where you can help me." Delia slipped back into her kitchen and returned a few minutes later with steaming cups of coffee. "Here you go. This will perk you up for some more lovemaking . . . if you want."

He sipped the coffee and was pleasantly surprised. "This is really good."

"I buy the best coffee from Brazil and I make it strong. I love strong things, Custis. Strong men, strong lovemaking, and strong characters in my novels. But like I said, I'm out of ideas except for one."

"And that is?"

"I want to write a series based on *you*. As promised earlier, I'll change all the names and give myself the freedom to embellish the true facts, but at least it will be based on a real frontier lawman and real accounts. My publisher thinks this is a wonderful idea and has encouraged me to try this so that my work becomes the standard of excellence. My work will be so much better than Beadle's or any other dime novelist that I'll put them to shame and out of business. If I do this right, I can become extremely rich . . . and you'll be well rewarded."

Longarm shook his head. "Delia, while I admire your

ability to write and create stories and the financial independence you've achieved, I honestly don't want to have anything to do with it."

She set her cup down and came over to stand before him. "I promised you I'd pay you well and that there would be other . . . offerings." Delia untied the little rope sash at her waist and opened the front of her bathrobe. "Do you *really* want to turn me down and miss out on so much that I am offering?"

Longarm put his cup of coffee down and stared at those luscious breasts. Even without conscious thought he could feel his manhood stiffening and his hand found the soft wetness between her thighs. Delia closed her eyes and sighed with pleasure.

"I could pass on the money," Longarm said in a thick voice, "because having a lot of money has never been my dream. But when it comes to the flesh . . . especially when it comes to someone as beautiful, willing, and desirable as you . . . I have feet of clay."

She reached down and stroked his stiffening rod. "It's not your feet that I'm interested in, Custis."

Longarm kissed her and led Delia back into her bedroom. For an instant, he eyed the swing seat, but then he decided he was too hungry to wait for her to adjust the contraption. So he just pushed her gently down on the bed and mounted her like a stud would a mare in heat.

Chapter 5

Longarm staggered into his office the next day at eleven o'clock and the first thing he did was to pour a cup of weak coffee. Ignoring Pete Schilling, he went over to his desk, opened the *Denver Daily News* that he'd just purchased, and immersed himself in the latest happenings.

"Long night?" Billy asked a short time later. "You look like you've been dragged through a knothole."

"You don't look so great yourself. You got something on your mind or did you just come over here to give me grief?"

"I have a job in Nevada that I want to send you on . . . that is, if you still want to work for me and not for Miss Delia Wilson providing her fodder for her sensationalist dime novels."

Longarm took a sip of the coffee. "Billy, you are a cheapskate. This coffee is so weak I can see the bottom of my cup."

"I need an answer about Nevada," Billy said. "Or should I send someone else?"

"You don't have anybody else worth a damn."

"Deputy Schilling has already offered to go and he looks up to it physically . . . which you don't."

"Pete isn't capable of wiping his own ass, much less doing any kind of job that would be a credit to this department."

"Oh, he's a little better than that," Billy argued. "And he knows that these long distance assignments are what brings a lawman a reputation. I think he is a little jealous that Miss Wilson isn't asking him to tell her some stories."

"What stories could Pete tell? How he shot himself in the toe when trying to learn how to do a fast draw? Or about the time he arrested a city councilman for a murder, then learning that the councilman had been in Pueblo on business at the time of the murder?"

"Well, everyone makes mistakes," Billy said, "and Pete really wants me to send him to Nevada."

"Pete would do anything to get out of Denver and away from that loudmouthed pig of a wife."

"Are we going to waste anymore time discussing Deputy Schilling or are you going to come to my office and find out what is going on in Nevada that needs immediate attention?"

"I'm coming," Longarm said, folding his newspaper and swilling down the remainder of his coffee. "Just don't rush me."

When they were inside of Billy's office, the man shut his door and motioned Longarm to take a chair. "Before we talk about Nevada, I want to know what is going on with Delia Wilson, the dime novelist."

"She's insistent that I give her some stories and promises to change the names and facts enough so that there won't be any fallout on you, me, or this agency."

"I don't trust her."

"Me, neither."

"Then I take it you declined her offer?"

"I tried, Billy. Honest, I really tried. But . . ."

"But she screwed you half to death, which is why you look so awful and came in so late this morning. Right?"

"Yeah, but . . ."

"Listen, maybe the best thing for you and me right now is to send you out of town."

"Sounds good to me."

"Glad to hear that. Get some travel money from Lola and we'll arrange for you to leave first thing in the morning. Tickets will be at the train station, same as usual."

"Thanks. But this time, give me enough travel money so that I don't have to hold a tin cup out in the aisle begging for pocket change. I need at least two hundred dollars if it looks like I'll be out of town for a few weeks."

"One hundred tops. You can wire me for more if you have good reason."

"Billy . . ."

"It's not my money . . . it belongs to our taxpayers and I'm not seeing it wasted on your insistence to debauch yourself."

"Tell me about Nevada."

"Our federal marshal in Reno was gunned down yesterday and his wife was shot three times and is barely clinging to life at the hospital."

"Someone shot Marshal Pierce and his wife, Agnes? Why?"

Billy threw up his hands. "No one knows. But the story gets even worse. Marshal Pierce and his wife have a sixteen-year-old daughter that was forcibly taken during the shooting."

"Where . . ."

"They were traveling in a buggy and on their way to Carson City when they were attacked by highwaymen. Apparently, the outlaws knew that Marshal Pierce had come into some money from an inheritance and was going to the Carson City Mint to buy some gold coins."

"Why didn't Pierce just put his money in a Reno bank?"

"I have no idea. I have a telegram and it doesn't give much in the way of details. But it seems that they shot our federal marshal and his wife from ambush and then took the money and the daughter. Got away clean and were clever enough to hide their tracks."

"I assume a posse was formed and gave chase," Longarm said.

"Sure. But the posse lost the trail."

Longarm shook his head. "I knew John Pierce very well and he was an outstanding lawman. His wife, Agnes, was a fine woman and I remember the daughter, Emily, as being a very bright and pretty girl."

"It was a terrible thing," Billy said. "Our office in Sacramento, California, is sending a marshal but my higher-ups want you to go as well."

"Why, is the man from Sacramento untested?"

"I have no idea." Billy leaned back in his chair. "It could be that by the time you arrive in Reno they will have caught the highwaymen and rescued the daughter and your trip will have been a waste of time and money. But we can't take the chance that the girl is still missing and that a federal officer and his wife were gunned down."

Longarm nodded. "I'll go back to my quarters and gather some things for the trip. If you will meet me at the station with a round-trip ticket and travel money, I still have time to catch this afternoon's train."

"Then do it. We all know that when a federal marshal is murdered, those responsible have to be swiftly brought to justice. And as for why they would take the Pierce girl . . . well, I have no idea. You say she was pretty?"

"Very."

"Then they may just have wanted to rape her before they killed her and buried the body where it would never be found."

"Or," Longarm added, "maybe they wanted to send her south into Mexico. There are rich people down there who favor blond hair and blue eyes and will pay a fortune for a pretty, virginal girl."

Billy sighed. "I had thought of that, of course, but the idea is so troubling that I just hope that isn't true."

"Better she is sold in Mexico than raped and murdered in Nevada."

"I suppose," Billy said. "But we owe Marshal Pierce and his wife everything in our power to save their daughter and bring the killers to justice."

"John Pierce was a fine man and outstanding marshal," Longarm said. "I've eaten at his table with his wife and daughter several times and I consider them to be friends."

"That's why I'm sending you instead of Pete Schilling," Billy admitted. "This is something we can't let pass. And if the killers have already been captured or killed, then we've wasted some time and money but we've at least given it our best effort."

"I'm on my way," Longarm said, coming out of his chair. "Just be at the station with the ticket and money and I'll make sure that justice has been swiftly and properly served."

"Maybe you should take Miss Delia Wilson along," Billy suggested. "She'd have to pay her own way, of course, but it would get her out of my hair."

"Bad idea," Longarm countered. "Real bad."

"She wants stories."

"That's right, she does. But we want justice and the two are not the same."

"I see your point." Billy stuck out his hand. "Good luck, Custis."

"Hey," Schilling called, hurrying up to Longarm. "You going to Nevada on that murder case?"

"That's right."

"I'd like to go along."

"Sorry. Maybe next time."

Schilling's face darkened. "I don't know why you get all the best assignments."

"I know why," Longarm said, "because I deliver and don't screw up."

Schilling's face reddened. "Maybe this time you'll meet your match and your maker. When that happens, I'll get to travel and build my own reputation."

"Building a reputation is the last thing a lawman wants or needs. But you wouldn't understand that, Pete, because you're not only arrogant but inept and stupid."

Before Schilling could reply, Longarm brushed past the man and headed out of the office. When he'd arrived less than an hour ago, he'd felt jaded but now with a mission in mind, he felt suddenly rejuvenated. John and Agnes Pierce had been a fine couple. And their daughter was the love of their lives. Now, the family had been destroyed along with their hopes and dreams.

Longarm stepped out of the Federal Building and pulled his hat down low. A cold wind was blowing out of the northwest and storm clouds were piling up over the Rocky Mountains. Reno would probably also be cold with snow . . . but perhaps not as much and he knew that down in Mexico, the days would be warm and sunny.

But he hoped he would not have to go that far because a pretty girl like Emily could disappear down there and never be seen or heard from again.

Chapter 6

"Going somewhere?" the voice in the hallway asked.

Longarm turned to see Delia standing by the door that he had forgotten to close. "Hello."

She stepped inside, eyes on his traveling bag stuffed with a change of clothes and a box of ammunition. "I would hate to think that you were running out on me after last night."

"I have to catch the four o'clock train up to Cheyenne."

She folded her arms across her chest. "Do you mind telling me why?"

Longarm finished stuffing his bag and then he said, "Come on in and close the door."

"From the expression on your face and the fact that you're preparing to leave town tells me that you aren't interested in making love right now."

"No, I'm afraid that I'm not," he admitted.

"You were just going to run out on me without a word of explanation after what we did most of last night?"

"I didn't have time to track you down," he said, knowing it sounded lame. "I would have sent you a telegram in a few days."

"I don't think so." She frowned and tried to hide her disappointment. "You're going out on an assignment. Are you going tell me about it?"

Longarm didn't think that Delia was hurt . . . but he wasn't certain. So far she seemed so matter-of-fact about their relationship and lovemaking. Passionate and energetic but not by any stretch of the imagination was she in love with him and feeling heartbroken.

"A lawman friend of mine and his wife were shot to death in an ambush on their way from Reno to Carson City. Apparently Marshal Pierce had come into a sizable inheritance. Maybe he had a friend or someone he trusted and wanted the man to invest his money in Carson City. I just don't know. But the couple was killed and their daughter abducted."

Delia's blue eyes widened. "I suppose I can understand the ambush if your marshal friend and his wife were carrying money . . . but I don't at all understand why robbers would take a girl."

"Me, neither. She's a real sweet kid."

"How old?"

"Fifteen or sixteen."

Delia shook her head. "Do you think they took her for their sexual pleasure and plan to kill and bury her?"

"I'm afraid that might be the case." Longarm shrugged into his heavy winter coat. "Marshal Vail suggested that they might want to deflower her and then take her down to Mexico to sell to some rich man who has a passion for young, blond American virgins."

"I have heard of that happening." Delia stepped forward and rested her arms on his shoulders. "I want to come."

"No," he said flatly. "The parents are dead and the chances of this turning out well for Emily are slim. This isn't going to be the kind of story you can turn into one of your dime novels."

"You're right. But it's a *real* story and one that might . . ."

He removed her hands and gently pushed her away. "Delia, do you really think that I'd allow you to . . . to sensationalize the murder of a girl's parents and then the tragedy of her being raped by a gang of outlaws and either killed or sold to someone down in Mexico?"

"Of course not, damnit! I'm all for making money, as I'm sure you've learned, but I'm not insensitive and callous. I want to help and I want to be a part of something that is real and important."

"Look, this is almost certain to turn out badly. Also, there's a fair chance that by the time my train arrives in Reno the outlaws will have been caught, sentenced, and hanged."

"But you have to go in case they got away and the girl is still alive."

"That's right. My boss also knew Marshal John Pierce although he'd never met John's wife and daughter. He wants the culprits caught and brought to justice almost as badly as I do."

"So this could be just a sad and unnecessary train trip."

"Exactly."

Delia walked over to face a mirror then pivoted around and said, "I don't suppose you'd be willing to telegraph me if the killers got away and the girl has not been recovered."

"I'm afraid I wouldn't," he confessed. "I'd be on the hunt."

"Then I'm coming. You can't stop me from buying a ticket and going with you, Custis. Last I heard this was still free country."

"You don't have time to pack or . . ."

"All I have to do is withdraw money from my bank and run to the train station and buy a ticket."

Longarm shook his head. "Delia, this isn't going to be a happy story. I wish that you would reconsider."

"We're wasting time," she said. "I'll see you at the station."

Before Longarm could protest or think of some argument that would keep the dime novelist here in Denver, she was gone.

Longarm reached under the bed and extracted a short and double-barreled shotgun that he'd recently acquired. He also found some extra shells. The shotgun had been made in Belgium and was of the highest quality. Also, because of its abbreviated barrel length, it was easy to carry on the train. He could always buy a used Winchester, but a shotgun like this would be impossible to find.

Billy had told him that there were at least three or four killers from the tracks they'd left at the murder site. Sometimes, a shotgun was the best equalizer a man could have on his side, and if Delia was going to insist on being a part of this hunt, he sure as hell wanted to have every advantage he could muster.

"You made it," he said as the train blasted its whistle to announce departure.

"I wouldn't miss this for anything," Delia said, holding a satchel, a briefcase, and a heavy coat. "This is going to be a great story."

"Even if the girl is dead?"

Delia had been about to climb onto the train's platform, but now she turned to him and said, "If she's dead, it will still be a great story . . . only a tragic one and tragedy sells. Remember William Shakespeare?"

"Yeah," Longarm answered. "And Edgar Allan Poe. They both reveled in tragedy."

"Correct." Delia jumped up on the platform as the train

lurched ahead with a bang and Longarm swung up beside her. "I hope you know what you're getting yourself into."

"I don't, actually," Delia replied. "But then neither do you."

Longarm nodded because she was exactly right.

Chapter 7

The Denver Pacific Railroad ran just over a hundred miles north up to Cheyenne. After a brief layover, Longarm and Delia boarded the Union Pacific heading west to Nevada. Because the sleeping compartments were small and Longarm was a big man, they had settled on separate compartments.

"I'll be doing some writing and I need to be alone with my thoughts," she explained. "But I'll enjoy being with you during meals and . . . well, if we want to make love."

"Sounds good to me," Longarm replied. He had decided that, if Delia was determined to go with him, he might as well enjoy it to the fullest. Making love on a narrow bed wasn't the best situation, but the rocking of the train was a motion that added an extra element to the sexual enjoyment.

"So," Delia said, the second day of their journey out Cheyenne, "tell me how many men you've tracked down and brought to justice in Nevada."

"I can't recall."

"Come on, now! Four? Five? Ten?"

Longarm stared out the window of the dining car. This was high desert country, almost waterless, and their next stop was Elko. "Maybe five."

"Which one was the most deadly?"

"There was a man named Red Sparks that was smart and cunning. He lured me into a mine up on the Comstock Lode and then he lit a stick of dynamite and blew up the opening intending to bury me alive. You see, he hated me so much he wanted me to die slow in the darkness of hunger and thirst."

Delia was writing fast on a pad of paper, filling it with notes. "How did you survive?"

"It was dim in the mine. I had gone in about a hundred feet looking for Red. When I realized he had somehow gotten behind me, I turned to leave but immediately saw a fuse burning near the mouth of the cave."

"But you were too far away to put it out."

"That's right, and so I ran deeper into the mine and rounded a corner just as the blast went off. The corner saved me from flying rocks."

"And?"

"And the blast didn't quite close the mouth of the mine so when the dust settled a little, I hurried up to a small opening of light. The rock dust was so thick I was choking, so I started pulling rocks away so I would have enough room to squeeze out of the mine."

"And?"

"I saw Red through that little hole in the rubble. He had a shovel and was fixing to close the hole and make sure I was buried alive."

"What a fiend!"

Longarm sipped at his coffee. The meal they had shared had been excellent. "Red was a sadistic killer. I heard him laughing as he pitched the first shovel load of gravel onto the hole. And just before he could put another shovelful in place, I jammed my Colt revolver through the hole and started firing as fast as I could . . . but I was shooting blind. There wasn't enough space for anything more than my hand and I knew that, if I missed, Red would chop off my hand with the shovel's blade, then finish burying me alive."

"But you *didn't* miss."

"No, I didn't," Longarm answered. "But I didn't quite kill Red. I was lucky enough to hit him twice . . . once in the side and another in the groin just about two inches below his belt. I heard Red screaming and knew that he was seriously wounded so I started clawing through the rubble as fast as I could. There was no doubt in my mind that Red would kill me if he could."

"And you had emptied the Colt?"

"Yes. I should have kept one bullet handy, but in my panic I did not."

"So what happened?"

"Well, I tore away enough rock and gravel to get my head and upper body out of the mine, but my damned cartridge belt and holster were hanging me up. Red saw me coming out of the rocks like a big snake and although he was mortally wounded, he had me dead to rights . . . stuck and helpless."

"So how did you survive?"

"I always keep a hideout, twin-barreled derringer," Longarm explained, showing Delia how his watch fob was soldered to the derringer. "I pulled my Ingersoll railroad watch out of my pocket and said, 'Well, looks like we're both going to die right about noon today. My comment caught him off guard and he cocked his head a little and smiled.'"

"He smiled?"

"That's right." Longarm took another sip of coffee. "And do you know what that son of a bitch said?"

"No."

"He reached down to unholster his six gun and drawled, 'It's way too nice a day for us to both die at high noon, so I'm going to kill you and then see if I can get to town and find a doctor.'"

"'Good idea,'" I told him as I slipped the derringer out of my pocket. When he saw the gun, he tried to bring his pistol up but he was too late."

"And you killed him on the spot?"

"Hell yeah, I did. Red was bad to the bone and I shot him twice in the face. It took me another five minutes to get out of that damn mine and I swore I'd never go back into another as long as I lived."

"Where is the man buried?"

"Carson City Cemetery. He got a far nicer funeral than he deserved." Longarm frowned. "I never understood why people pay their respects to a cold-blooded killer, but they often do."

Delia quickly scribbled some more notes and stood up. "I'm going to my compartment to write this into my story."

"Just change the names."

"I will. I promise. How long before we get to Elko?"

"I expect we'll roll in there in the next hour or two. They usually stay over for about an hour to take on wood and water."

"Let's meet when the train stops and take a look at the town."

"Not much to see. Just another railroad town. There are some big cattle ranches around here and the cowboys can get pretty rowdy."

"I'll expect you to protect me from any wild cowboys."

"I'll do 'er," Longarm promised, watching her leave.

When the train pulled into Elko, Longarm was taking

a nap and by the time he checked to make sure that Delia wasn't still on board most of the passengers had already scattered into the bustling railroad and ranching town. Longarm had been in Elko a number of times and when he began to look for Delia he could not find her.

The locomotive blasted its steam whistle and Longarm hurried back onto the train looking for Delia but she was still missing. Troubled, he stopped and asked the conductor if he had seen her get either on or off the train.

"I saw her get off, but she didn't get back on," the man said. "Wasn't she going with you all the way to Reno?"

"That was the plan."

"Well, either she changed her mind about Reno or else she'll just have to catch the next train through," the conductor mused. "Prettiest woman I've laid eyes on in quite a while."

"Oh, she's pretty all right. But she's also the kind that can get into trouble."

"I could see that," the conductor agreed.

Longarm had a decision to make and it had to be fast. "I can't leave Miss Wilson behind," he said. "She may be in serious trouble."

"Next train will be through tomorrow. Sorry you're leaving us."

"Me, too."

Longarm rushed to the compartment and collected his belongings. He jumped off the train as it was starting to roll and hurried back into town and began asking everyone he met if they'd seen a lovely young woman who'd gotten off the train.

Finally, a businessman in a brown derby hat said, "I saw people running to help a woman who'd been stabbed about twenty minutes ago. People were shouting and there was a lot of commotion. I don't know who the woman was or if she died or not. I caught a glimpse of her dress as they carried her off and it was blue."

"Where is the doctor's office!"

"Two blocks up on the left. Dr. Williams is . . ."

Longarm didn't wait to hear any more. Delia had been wearing a blue dress. What in the world could have happened!

Longarm found the doctor's office and burst into a back room to see Delia lying on a table, her blouse blood-soaked and pulled up under her breasts.

"What happened?"

The doctor whirled around, face angry. "Get out of here!"

"I'm a United States deputy marshal and this woman and I were going to Reno. How badly hurt is she?"

"She was stabbed but the blade ricocheted off her belt then gave her a nasty slice just under the ribs."

"Looks like she lost a lot of blood."

"Not that much," the doctor replied. "But if it hadn't been for that belt, she probably would be dead."

"I wonder if someone was intent on robbing her."

"I have no idea. She should come around soon. Maybe she can tell you exactly who did this to her."

"I hope so."

Ten minutes later, Delia did come around and found Longarm hovering at her side. "How are you feeling?"

"Hurts like hell."

"Did you see who stabbed you?"

"Yes. It was Frank Roman."

"And who is he?"

"He's a dime novelist that I met in Santa Fe."

Longarm waited for more and when it didn't come, he

asked, "So tell me why this dime novelist from Santa Fe wanted to kill you."

"It's a long story, Custis."

"We've missed our train and I've got nothing better to do than listen."

"I'm sorry about missing the train."

"We can catch another tomorrow if you're up to traveling."

"I will be."

"Tell me about Frank Roman the Santa Fe dime novelist."

Delia sighed. "It's not a story that I'm particularly proud of. I heard of him and went to Santa Fe looking for some writing advice. Frank is a man in his forties, single and looking for love."

"And you let him think you were that love so you could get him to help you start a career as a dime novelist."

"That's right. I didn't mean to sleep with him, but . . . well, he became very infatuated with me and promised to give me a few story ideas as well as introductions to his New York publisher and editor."

Longarm's eyebrows shot up. "You took his stories?"

"Yes, but I changed them a little."

"But not enough in Frank's opinion. Right?"

"Right. Anyway, he became very possessive and I tired of him after only a few days. When I tried to leave Santa Fe, he became enraged and said I'd used and deceived him."

"Which you did."

Delia nodded. "I didn't mean to hurt the man. I never intended to let things get out of hand."

"So when you left, he tried to stop you."

"Yes. And when he found out that I wouldn't change my mind and stay, he grew ugly and threatening."

"To kill you?"

"Yes. He was scary and I was afraid. I left on a stage in the middle of the night. I thought he'd get over me but I heard that he did not and had started drinking so hard that he couldn't write anymore. Last I heard, he was a raging wreck of a man." Delia grabbed Longarm by the shirt. "Custis, I swear that I didn't mean to hurt the man."

"Well, Delia, guess what? You not only hurt him but apparently ruined him and now he has come here to take his revenge. Seeing you with me probably didn't help."

"I'm so sorry!"

"Me, too," Longarm replied, feeling angry. "I don't need any more enemies. But the real question now is . . . is Frank Roman still here in Elko waiting for another shot at you and possibly me . . . or did he get back on the train and is he waiting to strike again in Reno?"

"I have no idea."

Longarm considered the situation for a few moments, then said, "Is Frank Roman a man who has guns?"

"He has a fine collection," Delia replied. "He's very proud of his guns and he also showed me a case full of trophies he's won in shooting competitions with both rifles and pistols."

Longarm groaned. "This story of yours gets worse by the minute. So we have a man capable of shooting us from a distance."

"I'm afraid so."

"Did he say anything to you when he stabbed that knife in your side?"

"Yes."

"What exactly did Frank Roman say?"

" 'Die, you coldhearted bitch.' "

"Well," Longarm said, "I suppose that is one of the lines he's used in his bloody dime novels."

"I'm not a woman easily frightened," Delia said, "but I have to tell you that Frank Roman is a man I wish that I'd never met."

"It's a little late for that," Longarm told her.

"So what do we do?"

"We get a room and some food and hole up until the next train west comes through Elko. Then, we board it and when we get to Reno we cover our backs and hope Frank Roman isn't hiding on some rooftop with a sharpshooter's rifle."

"I'm so sorry I messed things up like this."

Longarm was angry at Delia, but she didn't deserve to die for what she had done to Roman. And for that matter, neither did he.

Chapter 8

"So tell me," Delia began, as she propped up her pillow and sipped whiskey, "did you ever have to stand in the street and face a man who was faster with the draw than yourself?"

"Once for sure."

She reached for her pen and notebook. "Will you tell me about it?"

"I was sent to a small town named Monument, in southern New Mexico, because we got a telegram in Denver saying that the Otero brothers had gunned down the sheriff and had taken over the town. The brothers were outlaws known to raise hell on both sides of the border. It took me four days to reach Monument and when I rode in there wasn't anyone walking around on the streets."

"Did the brothers know you were coming?"

"I suspect that they knew someone was coming, but I sure didn't announce myself. I made certain that I rode in after dark and I put my horse up in the only livery in that dusty little town. The liveryman was an old coot who drank too much and smelled worse than any horse or mule.

He was angry but scared of the brothers and was forced into taking care of their horses without pay."

"Did he help you?"

"Yeah," Longarm said. "His name was Windy and it was a well-deserved nickname because he never stopped talking or farting. But he told me where the two brothers were drinking and that . . . drunk or sober . . . they were amazingly fast with their guns and damn good shots."

"So did you go straight away to find them?"

"I did. But I pinned my badge under my coat's lapel so that they wouldn't know I was a lawman. I went into the saloon and saw the brothers sitting at a back table drinking tequila. Each of them had a floozy on their lap."

"I imagine you were worried about the women being accidentally shot."

"That's right."

"So how did you handle it?"

"I asked the bartender to send the Oteros a couple of drinks on me. When he did it, I waved at the brothers like I was some old friend they'd met before. Then I walked over to them and struck up a conversation. They both spoke good English and I asked them if there were any other women in town as pretty as the ones they had sitting on their laps."

"Were there?"

"I don't know. One of the women was sober enough to realize that I might be a lawman. She said that in a laughing way but the Otero brothers didn't think it funny. I could see that they were edgy and explosive and I tried to think what I would do if they just drew their pistols and opened fire. I wanted to get those women out of the way of any harm.

"So what did you do?"

"I told the brothers I knew of a way to make some quick and easy money and wondered if they were interested. When they said yes, I told them that I needed to speak to them in private. One of the girls left, but the other was drunk and didn't want to go. I tried to grab her, and she latched onto my coat and damned if she didn't expose my badge under the lapel."

"Then all hell broke loose, I suppose."

"That's right. One of the brothers went for his gun, and knowing I couldn't beat him, I kicked out with my boot and knocked the man over backward in his chair, then drew my gun and killed the one still sitting at the table. Both women screamed, and one stepped in front of me so I couldn't get a clear shot to kill the one who was on the floor. He slithered out the back door, and by the time I was able to get there he was gone."

"Couldn't you have reached him in the back alley or wherever he went?"

"No, it was dark and I was worried that he was hiding and would kill me the minute I stepped outside. So I made sure that the one was dead and then I left the saloon and went back to the livery. Windy was waiting, and when I told him what had happened he said that all hell was going to break loose when the one that got away connected with his family living just across the border in Mexico."

"So," Delia said, "in a way, things suddenly became much worse."

"Yes, they did," Longarm agreed. "I had sort of stirred up a hornet's nest, and when the people of Monument found out what happened they nearly went into a panic."

"If they let just two banditos take over Monument maybe they didn't deserve to have a town."

"Well, you have to understand that Monument, New Mexico, wasn't much of a town at all. There were just a half dozen businesses and most of them depended on Mexicans who came peaceably across the nearby border to buy goods. So there were a lot of complications, but everyone knew that the Otero family was going to come to collect a body and that when they did they would be out for blood."

Delia was writing fast. "Sounds to me that even someone like you was in pretty far over your head."

"I was. I had to ride ten miles to find a telegraph office and I sent telegrams off to both Denver and Santa Fe explaining what I'd done and what I thought was going to happen. I don't often have to ask for help, but I did that time."

"Did help reach you?"

"No. And I was pretty sure that it wouldn't come in time so I stood out in the street and fired off my gun a few times and called for any man with a backbone to step out to talk. Windy was the first one to come join me but then some of the others who had buildings that they didn't want to be torched came out to see what I had to say."

Longarm's throat was getting dry so he took the bottle from Delia's hand and took a swallow. "How you feeling?"

"It hurts but the whiskey helps. I'll be ready to get out of here and get back on that train tomorrow. But finish your story about what happened in Monument, New Mexico."

"Sure. I stood in the street and told Windy and the others that it was clear the Otero family would return later in the day and that I could either leave them . . . or they could stand with me and fight. Really, Delia, I gave them little choice."

"So they found some backbone and stood with you?"

"That's right. And as luck would have it, a pair of Texas Rangers rode into town saying they'd heard of the fix we were in and had come running to help. They were good, lean fighting men, and they helped me position the townspeople and prepare them for an attack."

"When did the Otero men show up?"

"About sundown. There were nine, all armed to the teeth with bandoliers of bullets draped over their shoulders. Some even had swords and they were pretty fierce-looking. Windy, the rangers, and I stood in the middle of the street and faced them with at least a dozen townsmen hiding on rooftops and around corners of buildings. When I told the Mexicans to turn around and leave, they demanded the body of Jose Otero and I said two of them could dismount and recover the body, but then they had to leave and never return."

"What did they say to that?"

"The one who had gotten away from me the night before in the saloon cursed me and maybe he was still drunk because damned if he didn't go for his gun. Someone on a rooftop shot him off his horse. Three more tried to grab their guns and fight and they all died in a volley of bullets, some of which were mine and some of them belonged to Windy and the two Texas Rangers. The point is, four of the Otero family died in seconds with more bullet holes in them than a hunk of Swiss cheese. Those who were smart wheeled their horses around and raced, but some of the people of Monument weren't about to let them get away and maybe return someday when neither myself or the Texas Rangers were around."

"It sounds like it became a slaughter."

"I'm afraid that is exactly what it became. The townspeople, many of whom had been robbed, beaten, and insulted for days shot them all down as they rode up the street and by the time they were out in the clear not one Otero was still in the saddle."

"My gawd!" Delia whispered. "I never heard of that fight!"

"It's a true story. But those battles along the border happen all the time and this just happened to be one of the bloodiest."

"Did you stay long in Monument?"

"No. I rode up to Santa Fe and made a report that never became public. And I never went back to that town, but I heard a year or so ago that it was doing pretty well and that Mexicans and Americans alike never spoke of the Otero family again. I'm sure that the family had been a scourge on both sides of the border for years and no one was missing them at all."

Delia finished with the notes. "I'll put this into one of my stories and change the location to the Arizona border and all the names will be different."

"I'm counting on you to do that," Longarm said. "And right now I need a good description of this fella that stabbed you."

"He is pretty ordinary-looking. About five feet ten inches tall, sandy-brown hair, bearded, and he has a scar on his chin."

"How was he dressed?"

"When I knew him in Santa Fe he was a dandy. But after he went downhill, he became slovenly. It happened so fast out there that I barely had a chance to see him. I just had a glance before I felt this terrible pain and fainted. But I think he was dressed like a working man, heavy brown pants, wool coat, and dirty boots."

"That description isn't going to help me much."

"Are you going out to look for him now?"

"That's my intention."

Delia reached out. "Please don't leave me."

"I'll lock the door and leave you my pistol. If I can find him tonight and either kill or arrest him for attempted murder, we'll both be a lot happier."

"Be careful. He is a very determined and clever man."

"Are you sure that you can't remember anything more to help me spot him if he's drinking in a saloon or eating?"

Delia's brow furrowed with concentration. "One more thing."

"What's that?"

"Frank Roman always favored very powerful cologne. It was called . . . Wild Sage."

"I've used it . . . sparingly."

"Well John practically drenched himself in the stuff and I recall smelling it when he stabbed me."

Longarm shook his head. "I can't just go around smelling men in saloons, Delia."

"I understand. But if you get near him, you'll smell it. Also, he likes cigars and the bigger and blacker the better."

"I'll watch for a man with a scar on his chin and a stogie in his mouth and who smells like Wild Sage."

"That's right. If you find all three, it will be Frank Roman."

Chapter 9

Longarm stood just inside the door of the hotel and peered out into the street. There were just two or three saloons in Elko and the Stag Saloon seemed to be the most popular. The other two saloons were only a few doors away and much quieter.

When he thought about Frank Roman, Longarm conjured up the image of a tortured soul, a person who had been a successful dime novelist and probably regarded himself as at least a minor celebrity in Santa Fe. Then along had come this beautiful, conniving woman named Delia Wilson, the daughter of the governor of Colorado, seeking his valuable insight on how to write dime novels. How flattering that must have been and when Delia had poured on the praise and charm, poor Frank Roman became putty in her hands. He'd fallen in love with Delia and probably even imagined she might marry an older and not especially attractive man because she admired his intellect and creativity.

For whatever reason Frank Roman had fallen for Delia and given her his most precious secrets . . . his best story

ideas, and she had taken them and left the poor dime novelist feeling used, forsaken, and foolish. No wonder he had
been so consumed by hatred that he had gone to Denver
and then followed her on a train to this small Nevada cow
and railroad town. And at the very first opportunity when
Longarm had not been at Delia's side he'd attacked her
with a knife. Frank Roman must have thought that he'd
dealt her a fatal blow, but now he would be sure to know
that Delia was alive and resting in a hotel with another
man who happened to be a United States marshal.

Longarm paused a few more moments, asking himself
what he would do if he had been grievously wronged and
made to look like a lovesick idiot. He would never have tried
to kill Delia, but he would surely have felt she deserved the
worst possible tragedies in life.

Had Roman gotten on the train yesterday and fled town?
He might even have taken the eastbound back to Denver
and returned to Santa Fe to either drink himself to death
or perhaps try to resurrect his ruined literary career. Yes,
that was a possibility and it was the one that Longarm
hoped for. But more than likely, a man with that much
hatred would attack Delia again and again until she was
dead and he felt vindicated and that justice by his hand
had been served.

So, Longarm thought, Frank Roman was either still in
Elko waiting to strike again before the westbound train
left for Reno tomorrow, or he had already left and was
waiting for them in Reno.

It was time to step out into the dim streets of Elko and
enter the saloons and try to find the bitter and dangerous
man. Once found, he would arrest Frank Roman, but he
would write a note to the judge asking for leniency and
understanding.

Longarm stepped out onto the boardwalk and paused

in the shadows. When his eyes were adjusted to the poor light he moved silently down the boardwalk to the nearest saloon and slipped inside and studied the occupants. The bartender gave Longarm just a passing glance before filling a mug of beer for one of the patrons standing at the bar. There were only seven or eight other customers hunched over their drinks, all of them obviously cowboys or the owners of small businesses.

"Come have a drink," the bartender called. "Beer or whiskey?"

"Neither," Longarm said, backing out the door and heading up the street.

The Last Chance Saloon was a little busier and again Longarm stepped inside but did not move toward the bar or the other customers. He could see every customer clearly and none of them matched the description that he'd been given of Frank Roman. The bartender didn't notice him and Longarm backed out without a word and headed toward the Stag Saloon.

This saloon was crowded and far larger and fancier than its competitors. The bar was at least thirty feet long and ornately carved out of glistening oak wood. There were at ten tables where men sat drinking and playing cards and a piano player was pounding out a tune at the back of the building while several saloon girls danced with cowboys, railroad workers, and business owners. Nobody was drunk and nobody was being loud or unruly. Longarm had been in this saloon several times and knew that the owner ran honest card games and didn't water down the beer or whiskey.

"Beer?" the one of two bartenders wearing clean white aprons asked when Longarm sidled up to the bar, pulling the brim of his hat low over his eyes.

"Sure."

The bartender poured Longarm a tall mug of beer and deftly whipped off its foamy top. "Be ten cents."

Longarm paid the man and nodded in appreciation. The beer was good and he sipped it while his eyes roamed over the faces in the room. It didn't take him long to spot a man that matched the description that had been given him by Delia. Frank Roman was smoking a big cigar at one of the tables with three other men playing poker. There was a half-empty pitcher of beer on the table and the players were using dollar bills and coins instead of poker chips. From the look of the piles at each player's left hand, Longarm could see that Frank Roman was doing quite well. He might have lost his ability to write dime novels, but he was obviously still sharp enough to be an excellent poker player.

"Aren't you that marshal from Denver?" the bartender asked, coming back to join Longarm. "I think I've seen you in here before. I believe your name is Marshal Custis Long."

Longarm was annoyed. The last thing he needed was for Frank Roman to spot him before he could subdue the former writer. He put his back to the room, lowered his head, and hissed, "I'm about to arrest one of your customers for that stabbing that took place."

"You mean someone in here stuck that pretty woman earlier today? That was a terrible and dastardly thing to do! Is she going to recover?"

"Miss Wilson is doing fine, but unless you keep your voice down and let me do my job without blowing my identity, there could be a shooting right here in the saloon."

Finally, the bartender understood. He was a short, round man in his fifties with a gray beard and mustache. "Marshal," he said in a low voice, "we don't want any wild shoot-outs. Why, the mirror behind our bar is worth a thousand dollars and is irreplaceable. Which man are you after?"

Longarm didn't even turn his head around. "The one on that table playing cards and wearing a brown coat and derby. He's smoking a big cigar."

The bartender nodded slightly. "Okay, I see him. Anything I can do to help?"

"Yeah. Go over there and pretend to accidently slip and then fall across the table."

"What!"

"Knock everything to the floor. Money, beer, and cards. When the players start collecting it say you're sorry and will give them a free pitcher of beer. Then hurry back and tell me if my man is packing a six gun on his hip or if you see any other weapon."

"But those boys will be madder than hell at me."

"It doesn't matter," Longarm insisted. "As soon as you come back and tell me how he's armed, I'll walk over while they're picking up their cash and cards and make the arrest. It's the best chance we have of avoiding gunfire."

The bartender didn't like the plan, but under Longarm's steely gaze he decided against an argument. "All right. I sure hope this works, and I wish you could just go over there and get the drop on him."

"I'm certain that Frank Roman knows what I look like and would go for a gun before I could grab him," Longarm explained. "This way, when he's down on the floor grabbing his poker winnings he won't see me coming."

The reluctant bartender nodded and left after folding a white bar towel across his forearm. Longarm watched him weave his way through the crowd taking drink orders and passing comments and smiles. When he reached the table where Frank Roman was sitting, the bartender slowly turned as if to speak to someone then pretended to lose his balance and crash into the table, spilling cards, money, and drinks across the floor.

Frank Roman and the others shouted in anger at the bartender, who threw up his hands indicating that he was sorry about the accident. When the players dropped to the floor and began to collect their money, Longarm went into action. He hurried across the room and drew his pistol, crouched low, and stuck the barrel into Frank Roman's beard.

"You're under arrest. Don't make me kill you."

Roman froze, then his eyes lifted to meet Longarm's steady gaze. "I failed to kill the bitch, didn't I."

It wasn't a question but instead an admission of failure.

"That's right. On your feet."

"Not until I collect my winnings, Marshal Long."

"Where you're going you won't need them. Stand up!"

But Frank Roman didn't obey the command but instead reached into his pocket, pulled out a derringer, and tried to shoot Longarm in the foot.

"Shit!" Longarm growled, pulling the trigger of his Colt revolver and sending a bullet downward into the man's back.

The former dime novelist collapsed on the floor. Longarm tore the derringer from his hand and then turned Roman over on his back. "Why the hell did you go and do that!"

Roman's eyes fluttered. His lips moved as he struggled to speak through a bloody froth. Longarm gently leaned low placing his ear close in an attempt to hear Frank Roman's dying words.

"That bitch will ruin you, too, Marshal. I'll see you in a paradise especially reserved for lovesick . . . lovesick *fools*!"

Longarm dropped the man's derringer into his own pocket. He looked around the saloon where everyone stood frozen.

"This man is the one that stabbed the woman out on the sidewalk earlier today. His name was Frank Roman and not so long ago he was a popular dime novelist."

"I've read his books. He was good," a man nearby offered.

"I've read 'em, too," a cowboy said quietly as he removed his Stetson. "There are at least a dozen Roman dime novels in our bunkhouse. Is that really Mr. Frank Roman?"

"Yes," Longarm said.

"Why'd he go and stab that woman?" the cowboy asked, looking genuinely sad and perplexed.

"Long, tragic story," Longarm replied. "You men collect the man's poker winnings and add a little of your own to give Frank Roman a decent and respectful burial."

"He was a damned good writer," the cowboy said, more to himself than to anyone around him. "He created this cowboy character named Lightning Jack who was a great hero and . . ."

Longarm didn't want to hear any more about Frank Roman or his dime novel heroes. He had done what had to be done here, but as he stared down at Roman's body and the blood pool that was surrounding it, Longarm suddenly felt disgust and bitter regret.

"Take up the collection and put his name on a tombstone and under it the words, *he was a fine dime novelist.*"

"You think that's what he'd like to have carved on his tombstone?" someone asked.

"I'm sure of it," Longarm replied as he headed for the door.

Outside, he took a few deep breaths and then he headed down to a quiet saloon where a man could drink and not be bothered. Where Longarm could try to figure out what he might have done differently in order to save a ruined life that had once been celebrated in both cities and small ranching towns. And especially in isolated Nevada bunkhouses.

Chapter 10

"Delia," Longarm said, gently nudging her awake. "The train just pulled into town and it'll be taking on wood and water. I checked and it leaves for Reno in less than two hours. Thought you might want to get dressed and packed, then we can go find something to eat before we get on board."

She yawned and scrubbed the sleep from her eyes. "I feel a lot better today. And I'm so glad that you weren't hurt last night and were able to kill Frank Roman before he had another chance at me."

"Yeah," Longarm said quietly as he pushed the window curtain aside and looked down at the street. "It worked out, I suppose."

"What does the *suppose* mean?" she asked, sitting up and pushing a tendril of hair back from her face.

Longarm turned to face her. "I don't know. I didn't feel good about killing him."

"He stabbed me!" Delia said, voice rising. "Frank meant to kill me and he would have killed you as well."

"True, but he had what he thought were good reasons."

"Because I took some of his story ideas?"

"And used the man before you broke his heart."

Delia sat up in bed, covers falling to her lap, breasts exposed. "Custis, are you worried that I'm going to do the same thing to you? Is that what this is about?"

"No," Longarm told her without hesitation. "I'm not Frank Roman and I have no illusions about who you are and the lengths that you will go to in order to get what you want."

He thought she was going to explode, but then Delia took a deep breath and relaxed. "Custis, I told you that I only wanted stories to use for my future dime novels and that I'd change all the names. I don't see what that has to do with Frank Roman."

"I had to kill him, didn't I?"

"Come here."

Longarm went over to stand by the bed. "What?"

She began to unbuckle his cartridge belt and then his pants. "I think we need to have a little lovemaking before we leave this hotel room."

Longarm shook his head. "That isn't going to change how I feel about what happened to Frank Roman."

"Screw Frank Roman! He was an arrogant, difficult, and self-inflated man who used and discarded women and then couldn't stand being used and discarded himself. He stabbed me and you shot him dead. He would have tried to kill someone else so you did the world a favor by putting the man out of his misery."

Longarm shook his head but Delia was already in his pants and when she pulled him closer to the bed she rolled over and took him into her mouth.

Damn, Longarm thought, *I'm no stronger than Roman had been when she starts to do what she does so well.*

Five minutes later he was between her legs and they were lost in the pleasure of lovemaking. Longarm rode her gently, not wanting to hurt her because of the knife wound. But when he was a too gentle, Delia bit his earlobe hard and whispered, "Stop treating me as if I'm breakable! Come on and do me harder!"

Longarm was all too happy to grant her wishes. And when he roared and slammed his seed into her beautiful body, he made up his mind that she was a poison that he dared not take much longer or just like with Frank Roman, the results could be fatal.

The remainder of their train trip to Reno was uneventful. Delia was a little pale from the loss of blood but in high spirits. She had never been to Reno or the famous Comstock Lode and wanted to see them as soon as possible.

"The Comstock mines are mostly played out," Longarm explained. "The bodies of gold and silver under Virginia City and Gold Hill were discovered in the sixties and seventies and now all of Sun Mountain is honeycombed with mine shafts and tunnels. There hasn't been a huge ore discovery in at least a decade."

"I've read about what the Comstock was like in its heyday," Delia said. "It was a wild place."

"Wild and dangerous," Longarm added. "Over on the western slopes of the Sierra Nevada mountains the Forty-Niners panned gold out of streams and rivers. But when all the placer gold had been panned out the Comstock Lode was discovered and the same miners raced over the Sierras. Arriving on the Comstock Lode they found that there were no rivers or streams or any kind of good drinking water. No tall ponderosa pines, either. Instead, Sun Mountain is barren with just a few scrawny piñon and juniper pines scattered among the rocks and sage."

"So the Forty-Niners who had become accustomed to panning gold out of the streams couldn't pan anymore?"

"That's right. Some hammered short tunnels and shafts

into the rocky mountainsides but they hadn't a prayer of reaching the big underground ore bodies with mere picks and shovels. That meant they had to lose their precious independence and hire on with the rich mine owners who were building steam hoisting works and drilling deep shafts straight down through the hard rock. The miners found themselves being herded into wire cages and lowered hundreds of feet into the belly of the mountain, then working in dim tunnels that branched off the main shaft."

"It sounds like it was a brutal existence for miners."

"It was," Longarm said, "but the miners formed unions and they made good money. A lot of them died deep underground when their picks broke into underground reservoirs of boiling water or the tunnels collapsed. Even so, the hard rock miners kept arriving from all over the world. I didn't see the Virginia City in her prime, but even ten years ago it was a sight to behold. On C Street there were no less than fifteen saloons, and all of them were packed day and night. They have a big opera house and some amazing mansions."

"I want to see it all," Delia told him. "Even if Virginia City has gone bust."

"Well," Longarm said, "you can do your sightseeing while I look to find out who murdered federal marshal John Pierce and his wife and who abducted their daughter, Emily."

"You don't really think you'll find her still alive, do you?"

"I'm an optimist," Longarm replied. "Emily was young and beautiful and she would bring a steep price down in Mexico."

Delia nodded. "I can't even imagine a girl like that being taken into slavery and sold as a concubine for sexual pleasure."

"It's not a pretty picture, but if that did happen, then there is a chance I can find her."

"Even if you have to go into Mexico where you have no authority?"

"Yes," Longarm said, "even if I have to go deep into Mexico."

"I don't think I want to go there," Delia decided. "I would be afraid of what might happen."

"I'm glad to hear that," Longarm told her. "Mexico is a very hard and dangerous country. Down along the border there are bandits and raiding Apache. There are all kinds of people who would kill just for pleasure on both sides, and it's no place for a woman like you."

"You mean a woman with my looks."

"That's right. You'd attract way too much attention with your blond hair and beautiful face. If I have to cross the border, I'll try to be as inconspicuous as I can, and I damn sure won't tell anyone I'm a federal marshal because that would be needlessly putting a death warrant on my head."

"So if you decide to ride south to the border, I'll have to decide where I'm going to stay if you return with or without that girl."

"Exactly."

Delia patted his thigh. "Well, I'll make that decision when I come to it. The beauty about being a dime novelist is that I can write anywhere I stay."

"You should have stayed in Denver."

"If I had," Delia shot back, "Frank Roman would have killed me by now."

Longarm agreed. Looking out the window he studied the stunted sage and the long, white stretches of salt and alkali flats. "Nevada is probably the bleakest landscape in the entire West. It has very little drinkable water and the summers are scorching hot while the winters can be bitterly cold. The wind blows across Nevada as hard as it does across Wyoming and Montana."

"How much farther is it to Reno?"

"We should reach it in about four hours."

"Is it as ugly as Elko and some of these towns we've passed today?"

"No," he said, "Reno is beautiful. It's situated at the base of the Sierras and the Truckee River runs right through town. Reno is smaller than Denver but a major city because of the railroad and all the mining and timbering in the area. You'll find it pleasing to the eye."

"Nice restaurants and hotels?"

"Very nice."

"Then maybe if you decide to go to Mexico I'll spend a while in Reno."

"That wouldn't be a bad idea. There are daily stagecoach rides up to the Comstock Lode. It's something not to be missed."

Delia smiled. "Let's just see where the cards fall after we arrive and then we can both make our decisions."

"Wouldn't have it any other way," Longarm said, watching a skinny coyote trot across a ridge of stunted sage and broken rock.

Chapter 11

When their train reached Reno, Longarm and Delia had found a hotel beside the Truckee River and then enjoyed a fine dinner in the dining hall. They made love and slept well that night. In the morning both took baths and gave their soiled clothing to the hotel maid to be washed and dried.

Longarm buckled on his gun and cartridge belt, then prepared to meet the local sheriff and get updates on the murder of federal marshal John Pierce and his wife and the abduction of their daughter.

"I'd like to be in on that meeting," Delia said, slipping into her coat.

"I don't think that would be a very good idea."

"Why not?"

"Because what the sheriff here has to say might be confidential and I'm sure he'd rather not discuss the case with a dime novelist who might use it in one of her future novels."

"Then don't tell him I'm a writer."

"What would I tell him? That you're my curious and beautiful lady friend? I doubt that would go over very well."

Longarm picked up his Stetson. "Let's be straight about something, Delia. I've enjoyed your company very much so far, but the real reason you're coming along is that you are the daughter of Colorado's governor. That won't carry much weight here in Nevada. In fact, it won't carry any weight at all."

Delia didn't like hearing that and it plainly showed on her lovely face. "I could help you with this . . . if the trail doesn't lead to Mexico."

"And how, exactly, would you do that?"

"Because I've written so many violent scenes in my dime novels I have a unique way of looking at crimes."

Longarm almost laughed out loud. "Do tell!"

"Yes, I really do. And, I have more money than you and sometimes money can be used to obtain information that could not be gotten in any other way."

"I'll keep that in mind," Longarm replied. "Are you going to take a stage up to Virginia City today?"

"Not today. I'm planning on looking around the town and taking some notes to use in a future novel. Also, I wouldn't dream of leaving until you've told me what you learn this morning about the Pierce family."

"Delia, please don't start asking questions about the murders and Emily's disappearance. I want to be able to move around and dig up my own information and I don't want you to muddy the waters before I have a chance to reach some solid conclusions."

"Perhaps the sheriff has already found the girl dead . . . or alive."

"I hope he's found her alive and well," Longarm answered. "If that is the case, I still need to make sure that justice is served. Marshal Pierce was a federal officer and I can't allow his murder or that of his wife to go unsolved."

"Understood. Can we meet for lunch?"

"Make it dinner," he told her. "I'll be back here before dark."

"You will unless someone recognizes and tries to ambush you like they did Marshal Pierce and his poor, dead wife."

Longarm knew where the sheriff's office was located and he wasted no time with breakfast although a strong cup or two of coffee was in order. When he entered the office, he recognized Sheriff Tom Quinn from an earlier visit and recalled that they had worked well together. Sheriff Quinn young for the job, probably not yet out of his twenties. He was handsome and not especially bright, but tried his best to keep law and order in Reno. People liked Tom Quinn because he was always smiling and congenial, but Longarm had his reservations about the man's dedication or willingness to do any serious investigative work.

"I expected you to come in on the train yesterday," were the first words out of Quinn's mouth. He picked through the papers on his desk and found a telegram. "Your boss, Marshal Vail, said that you would arrive yesterday."

"I had a little trouble in Elko," Longarm replied glancing around the office and spotting a pot of coffee on the man's stove. "Any of that left?"

"Sure, help yourself, but you probably remember that I like my coffee hot and strong like my women."

Longarm found a reasonably clean cup and poured coffee. He tasted it and found it to his satisfaction. "I remembered that you made a good pot."

"And I recall you smoke damn good cigars."

Longarm got the hint and gave the man a cigar, then took one of his own and when they were settled and smoking he said, "You're looking good, Tom. Better than I thought you'd look given the murders and the disappearance of the Pierce girl."

"I'm pretty sure that we've already caught the ambusher."

Longarm's cup of coffee stopped halfway to his lips. "Really?"

"That's right. I was leading a posse four days ago when we came upon a man that was considered a strong suspect in the murders. He had more cash than he should have and his rifle had recently been fired."

"Any other proof and did he say what he did with Emily Pierce?"

"No," Quinn said, suddenly looking away. "I brought him back here and tossed him in jail. There was a crowd outside that grew big and angry. It became a lynch mob around midnight."

Longarm glanced at a back door that he figured stood between them and a few cells. "I'm sorry to hear that. How many deputies do you have working for you?"

"None. The damned city cut my budget to the bone and I'm all on my own for the time being."

"I have a feeling this story is going to get worse."

"I'm afraid so." Quinn drew deeply on the cigar and blew a cloud of smoke up toward the ceiling. "I had a shotgun in my hands when I faced the lynch mob just outside the front door and I made it clear that no one was going to get past me. I told the mob that the man I'd jailed would go before a judge and jury and have a court of law decide his fate based on the very strong evidence we'd already confiscated."

Longarm nodded with understanding. "I take it that the evidence you were referring to was the cash presumably taken from Marshal Pierce after he and his wife were ambushed."

"That's right. Only it wasn't nearly as much cash as we'd expected."

"How much?"

"One hundred and sixty dollars."

Longarm shook his head. "From what I've been told, Marshal Pierce had a great deal more money that he was taking to someone in Carson City."

"True, but I figured the suspect had been smart enough to stash most of the money and planned to pick it up after things quieted down."

"So how do you know the money had been taken from Marshal Pierce?"

"Well," Quinn said, "this suspect's name was Dub Robertson and he was a known thief and cattle rustler."

"Being a thief and cattle rustler is a long ways from being a murderer."

"That's right," Quinn admitted. "But Robertson had blood on the cuffs of his shirt and bloodstains on his boots. When last seen a few days earlier, he'd been dead broke and drunk as usual. When we overtook Dub Robertson he had a good horse and saddle as well as a Winchester and new Colt revolver with several boxes of ammunition."

"Were the weapons recognized as belonging to Marshal Pierce?"

"No, but a man with lots of stolen money could buy weapons any place, no questions asked. I'm sure we had the ambusher but he was sober enough to keep his silence. In fact, he surprised us by asking for a good lawyer."

"So, what's he saying now?"

The sheriff sighed and shook his head. "He isn't saying anything."

Longarm placed his cigar down and sat up a little straighter in his chair. "Sheriff, I'm starting to think that Dub Robertson isn't around anymore."

"I'm afraid that's right. While I was out in front that night holding a lynch mob at bay, someone snuck around behind the jail in the alley, struck a match, and shot Dub Robertson to death in his cell. Before I could circle around and try to capture the shooter, he galloped away in the night."

"You left the cell window *open*?"

"It was barred and not too cold. Dub didn't complain and with all the trouble I had my hands filled with, I just forgot to shutter down that window so that no one could peer through the bars."

Longarm swore in frustration.

"Yeah, it's not good. The judge was furious. He'd been expecting a huge trial and lots of publicity and he's running for his office again so that would have played right into his reelection campaign."

Longarm came to his feet and began to pace back and forth. "So we still don't have any idea where Emily Pierce is? Or if she is even alive?"

"That's right. Dub Robertson died with his secrets. But I'll tell you this . . . men have been searching the hills and valleys for fifty miles in all directions."

"But they never found poor Emily?"

"They weren't looking for the girl although I was hoping they'd find her alive," Quinn said. "They were looking for the money they figured Dub had hidden."

"What a mess."

"I know, but at least the killer is dead."

"Is he?" Longarm challenged. "How do you know for sure that Dub Robertson didn't rob someone else?"

"Because no one came forward telling me they were robbed."

"Maybe they didn't because Dub killed them instead of the Pierce family."

"Damnit, Custis! Don't you dare mess this up any worse

than it already is. I've had it up to my eyeballs with all of this and as far as I'm concerned and except for that poor girl, this case is closed."

"Not by one hell of a long ways it isn't," Longarm countered. "Not even close, Tom. We don't have any proof at all that Dub Robertson killed John and Agnes Pierce, then abducted their daughter."

"But . . ."

"Think hard, Tom! If it was Dub, where is the girl?"

"Probably buried in a shallow grave."

"Maybe, but maybe not."

"Did you come here just to make my life even more miserable than it has been this past week?"

"I don't give a damn about how miserable your life has been. All I care about is that we get the right man and find out what happened to Emily Pierce. She might be still alive."

"Highly doubtful."

"But possible."

Sheriff Quinn's upper lip curled and he jumped out of his chair. "I haven't had breakfast yet and I'm feeling a little queasy in the guts. You want to join me? I'm buying."

"Sure," Longarm said. "But a free platter of ham and eggs isn't going to change my thinking."

"Never thought it might," Quinn said, mashing his cigar out and marching over to pull on his hat and coat. "But I see no sense in beating a dead horse or wasting time chasing ghosts."

Longarm had to bite back a response. It was clear that Tom Quinn wanted nothing more than to put the murders and the kidnapping far behind him. Maybe he was up for reelection, too.

Chapter 12

Longarm finished his breakfast and folded his napkin. "Well, Tom, I'd best get busy."

"At what?" The sheriff wasn't pleased. "So are you going to go around my town sticking your nose into things and trying to make me look like a fool in my own town?"

"Not at all," Longarm replied. "You're a good lawman and the last thing I want to do is to cause you any embarrassment."

"In that case, get back on the eastbound train and go home to Denver. Tell Billy Vail that the killer of United States Marshal John Pierce and his wife, Agnes, is dead."

"And what do I say about thcir missing daughter?"

"Tell Billy that she is dead, too."

"I can't do that yet," Longarm replied.

"And I can't help you out," Quinn snapped. "I'm the only lawman in this entire town right now and it's a job too big for one man. I'm up late every night stopping barroom fights and Reno is going to explode if I don't get some help soon."

"I'm sorry about your situation," Longarm said, meaning it. "Reno is way too big for you to handle alone and the city council or the mayor is wrong to put the entire responsibility on your shoulders."

"Yeah, they are. So you can understand how the last thing I need to hear from you is that you think Dub Robertson might not have been the ambusher."

"Look, Tom. You have your job to do and I have mine. I promise you that I won't step on any toes or cause you any embarrassment. But you're too good a lawman to let this slide. If there's a chance that the murderer or murderers of John and Agnes are still on the loose, I'm sure you want to know about it. And if that girl—"

"She's dead or wishes she was dead," Quinn interrupted, cutting Longarm off.

"You're probably right, but I'm not leaving Reno until I know for certain."

They both stood up. Quinn tossed some money on the table and followed Longarm out the door. On the boardwalk the sheriff said, "Look, you're right about wanting to make certain that Robertson was the killer and abductor. And maybe I was a little hasty in closing the book on this, but it makes sense to me that the guilty man died in my jail cell by one of the members of that lynch mob."

"Did you ever consider that Dub Robertson was shot to death in order to cover up the truth?"

Quinn ran his hands through his graying hair and replaced his hat. "Just keep me posted on what you find, okay? And when you leave, I'd like to think that we'll still be friends."

"I'm sure we will be," Longarm told the man before walking away.

Longarm didn't make his presence all that obvious as he moved about the bustling town. He kept his badge hidden and when he entered business establishments he pretended to be a customer and then casually dropped remarks about the Pierce family. It was surprising how many of the townspeople wanted to talk about those killings and the missing Pierce girl. On his fourth visit to a local business Longarm finally got a good, solid lead.

The man who owned the biggest feed store in town was named Howard and he became impassioned when Dub Robertson's name was raised. "Robertson was a drunk, a whoremonger, and a pickpocket. I never thought he'd have the stomach for murdering a federal marshal and then kidnapping the man's daughter. God only knows how much she suffered at his hands. Robertson had a good woman, but I never could figure out why she put up with his drunken rages."

"He had a wife?"

"No, I said a woman. And Shirley isn't a whore, either. She's a fine woman, not much to look at but she goes to my church and she's been through hell. I think she believed that she could save Dub Robertson's soul if she kept working on him and she actually did drag him to church a few weeks ago."

"What does she do?"

"Besides trying to save lost souls? She's a seamstress and does pretty well at it. Shirley Morton's first husband owned the livery but he was no good. Dub Robertson wasn't a damn bit better. Some women just seem to feel bound and determined to save the worst of mankind."

"Yeah, I expect you're right about that," Longarm said, thanking the man for his time before leaving.

Five minutes later he entered the small business owned by Shirley Morton. Her shop wasn't much bigger than the interior of a stagecoach and it was piled high with shirts, pants, coats, and all kinds of dresses needing attention.

Longarm saw Miss Morton bent over stitching the hem of a gown.

"Can I help you, mister?"

"Maybe." Longarm had thought about what he would say to this woman and had decided that, if he really wanted any valuable information on Dub Robertson, he needed to be honest and forthright.

Shirley Morton was probably in her late thirties and she might have been pretty at half her age but time and long hours bent over her sewing had quickly aged her. Her hair was tied at the back of her head in a bun and she wore spectacles. Her face was lined and pale and she carried a definite air of weariness about herself and her tedious livelihood.

"What do you need fixed and how soon do you need it?" she asked, returning to her needlework. "Unless it's just a little repair, I can't get anything done for you in less than four days."

"I don't need anything mended, Miss Morton. I want to talk to you about Dub Robertson."

Her body stiffened and she looked up at him through the spectacles. "And who might you be?"

Longarm showed her his badge. "I'm a federal officer from Denver and I've come all the way out here to find out who killed Marshal Pierce and his wife and who took their girl."

"She wasn't a 'girl' anymore. She was a woman in every way."

Longarm tried to figure out if he was reading the statement correctly. "Are you saying she had known a man?"

"She was a Jezebel." The woman's voice hardened with hatred. "Oh, Emily came off as a real sweet, innocent little thing, all godliness and goodness." Shirley's eyes flashed. "But Emily was a scheming, conniving little harlot!"

If there had been room for a chair, Longarm would have collapsed into it. He chose his next words carefully. "Miss Morton, Emily was just sixteen and the daughter of a United States marshal. Everyone that I've talked to about her said that Emily was a lovely young girl."

"Woman! She was not a girl, Marshal, and I don't care what anyone said about her because she was a conniving slut."

"All right," Longarm said slowly. "So how do you know that?"

"She liked to seduce men. Men who couldn't see anything past her prettiness. Oh, she was real good at being coy and a seductress. I could name you at least three married men whose lives and marriages Emily ruined."

"Tell me their names."

"No." Shirley Morton took a deep breath and let it out slowly. "I will not speak anymore of the dead and the wicked. Emily is in hell now and that is justice enough."

"Did Dub Robertson love Emily?"

The question was not one that Longarm had given thought to; instead it just popped out of his mouth and once asked could not be taken back.

"He did, years ago."

"But he stopped loving her?"

"Yes, he broke free from her evil spell and came to love me and the Lord."

"Miss Morton, people tell me that Dub Robertson was a drunk and a thief. So . . ."

"Dub was fighting the Devil every day, but he was winning his battle and comin' around. We were going to get married as soon as he got baptized and completely accepted Jesus as his savior. He wasn't there yet, but he was moving that way. He had the makin's of a good, honest man, but then the sheriff found him with money and figured he was the killer that shot the Pierce family and took that Jezebel. But my Dub came by the money honestly."

"He was carrying almost two hundred dollars. How could a man drunk come by that much money?"

Shirley Morton's lower lip began to tremble and then tears slid down her cheeks. She sobbed and covered her face.

"I'm sorry," Longarm said quietly. "I didn't mean to upset you so badly. I'm just trying to find out the truth."

She used a cotton rag to dry her tears and then turned to look up at him and say, "I gave Dub that money."

"You?"

"Yes. He was on his way to Carson City to buy me a sewing machine and an engagement ring. And he would have done it, too, if that ignorant sheriff and his bloodlusting posse hadn't come upon my Dub and charged him with murder and abduction."

Longarm stared at the woman's face. "I don't suppose you have any way to prove what you just said."

"I got something."

"What?"

The seamstress slowly rose out of her chair and turned to a desk littered with her business paperwork. She rummaged around for a few minutes and then found a scrap of paper. "Here," she said, shoving it at Longarm. "Here is a paper showing you the sewing machine that he was going to buy. And as for the engagement ring . . . well, Dub wanted to surprise me so I don't know what it was going to look like or where he'd planned to buy it. But there's a fine jewelry store in Carson City and the man who owned it told Dub that he would get him something real special for me."

"Do you happen to know his name or the name of his jewelry store?"

"Sure. It was the Mint Jewelry Store and Mr. Elias Tea-garden is the owner. Dub told me that he was making a gold ring special for me with a real diamond. It was a small stone, but Mr. Teagarden swore it was of good color and high quality. I didn't want anything big and gaudy even if we could have afforded it."

Longarm read the little paper ad showing a sewing machine and noted the merchant's name in Carson City. He looked up and asked, "Did you tell Sheriff Tom Quinn about this?"

"What good would it have done? They'd already decided that my Dub was the killer and a few pieces of paper weren't going to change his mind. Dub was tried and sentenced to die before he even saw a judge or jury. I visited him for a few minutes in the cell and Dub was crying and telling me that he loved me and didn't do the crimes he'd been accused of. He begged me to get him a lawyer and I swore I would spend every penny I had ever saved . . . but they murdered him that night instead of lynching him."

"Can I keep this ad for the sewing machine?"

"Sure. My money is gone now along with Dub and everything else. I don't care anymore about anything except Jesus and God and justice."

Shirley Morton suddenly reached out and grabbed Long-arm by the coat. Her hands were blue-veined but strong and her voice was even stronger. "Are you going to prove to everyone in this town including that damned Sheriff Quinn that they got the wrong man killed?"

"If Dub Robertson was the wrong man, I will discover the truth and tell everyone."

Shirley Moore looked deep in his eyes. "If you find out who really killed that husband and wife, then you'll find the girl and I wouldn't be at all surprised if she and the killer were off somewheres spending all the family money and laughing about how poor Dub Robertson died for their crime."

"I will uncover the truth," Longarm promised.

"See that you do."

"Just one thing before I go."

"Spit it out."

"Don't tell anyone what you've just told me or that I'm a lawman. And if you have any idea of who Emily was seeing just before her disappearance, then tell me right now."

"Maxwell Pennington. He owns a gold mine up in Virginia City but it is my understanding that the mine hasn't produced very much in the last five or six years."

"Are you sure that Emily Pierce was seeing that man?"

"As sure as I know Emily Pierce is either in hell or on her way."

Longarm nodded and left the woman with his mind all awhirl.

Chapter 13

Longarm and Delia were well into their second bottle of French merlot and their empty plates had been removed. "Mind if I smoke?" Longarm asked.

"Of course not. Just please don't blow the vile vapor into my face."

"Wouldn't dream of it, Delia. So tell me more about your first day in Reno."

"I like this beautiful city. It has some very nice ladies' shops and I enjoyed a wonderful lunch by the riverfront. It was a little nippy, but still pleasant."

"Glad to hear that."

"And what about you?" she asked. "I'm assuming you didn't wander around shopping and sightseeing. Tell me what you found out about the murders and the abduction of the girl. Has she been found, yet?"

"No, she hasn't." Longarm emptied their bottle, leaned back in his chair, and told Delia about how they'd arrested Dub Robertson, who was carrying a suspicious amount of cash and then how the man had been shot through the back bars of his jail cell.

"Before he could even tell them what he'd done to that poor girl? How tragic!"

"It might be even more tragic than it is already."

"What do you mean?"

Longarm tapped the ash from his cigar into a silver ashtray. "I met a woman, a seamstress actually, who loved Dub Robertson and swears that she had given him money to go to Carson City and buy her an engagement ring and a sewing machine."

Delia's eyebrows arched upward. "This woman *paid* the killer to buy her a ring?"

"Yes. And a sewing machine."

"Well," Delia said with a faint smirk on her lips, "I'll have to give it to the seamstress for coming up with an original story."

Longarm extracted the ad for the sewing machine and showed it to Delia. "I found myself actually believing the story."

"You did?"

"Yes. If you had been there with the seamstress and seen her tears, seen her face and how she reacted, I think you would have believed her as well. As a matter of fact, why don't you pay Miss Shirley Morton a visit at her shop and see if you have the same reaction?"

"Give me directions and I'll do that."

"I will." Longarm blew a cloud of smoke over their heads. "And Miss Morton told me something else that was pretty shocking."

"I'm all ears, Custis."

"She claims that the sixteen-year-old Pierce girl was a seductress and nothing like the innocent virgin she portrayed herself to be."

"A federal marshal's daughter is seducing men?"

"Married men and single. Apparently, her latest conquest is a mine owner that lives up on the Comstock. His name is Maxwell Pennington."

"Oh, come on! Surely you don't believe that."

"I don't know what to believe," Longarm admitted. "But I intend to check out the stories. I will go to Carson City first and see if the jeweler or the merchant who was supposed to deliver a sewing machine to Dub Robertson even exist. If they do and what Miss Morton says checks out, then I'll go on up to Virginia City and pay a visit to Maxwell Pennington."

"It seems like a long shot to me."

"Maybe it won't after you meet the seamstress. I'm telling you, Delia, the woman is a real Christian and she is heartbroken. She really loved Dub Robertson and felt that she could save his soul and make him into an honest man and loving husband."

"Perhaps she has been trapped in her little shop far too long."

"Go see her first thing in the morning," Longarm urged. "But my mind is made up and I'm going to take a stage to Carson City tomorrow."

"I want to go with you even if I still don't believe the seamstress." Delia thought hard a moment and said, "But what about the girl? The so-called seductress? What . . ."

"I have no idea if she is dead or alive. I think that my only thread to follow in this case is to pay a visit to the mine owner. Miss Morton said that his mine was not producing much gold anymore."

"And I don't think you paying the man a visit will produce anything, either."

Longarm smiled and shrugged his broad shoulders. "It's the only lead I have so I'll follow it."

"Did the sheriff say if he tried to find out who shot the suspect through his jail bars?"

"No, he didn't."

"Well, don't you think that he should have tried to bring that man to justice?"

"I most certainly do." Longarm frowned. "Actually, something isn't right there but I have no idea what it is."

"Is the sheriff honest or was he just hoping that someone would shoot Dub Robertson so that it would save the city the cost of jail and a trial?"

"Again, I'm not sure."

Delia leaned back in her chair. "Sounds like you stirred up a whole lot of questions without answers."

"Goes with the territory," Longarm replied. "Sometimes getting to the truth is like peeling an onion one layer at a time."

"Can I use that metaphor in my next dime novel?"

"Why not?"

Delia stood up. "Let's go for a little walk to get some fresh air and then let's go to bed and get some real exercise."

"I like the way you think, Delia. I really do."

She took his arm. "If the light is on in the seamstress shop, I'll go in and have a word with her."

"She might not be willing to talk to you."

"She talked to you, didn't she?"

"Only after I showed her my badge. What are you going to show her?"

"Money."

"Might work," Longarm said.

"Can't hurt to try," Delia added as they started up Virginia Street.

Chapter 14

It was almost noon and Longarm and Delia were waiting for a stagecoach leaving for Carson City. The day was fair, cool, but sunny with bright blue skies. Longarm decided it was a fine day for traveling the roughly thirty miles between the two busy Nevada towns.

"So what did you think of Miss Morton and what she had to say?" Longarm asked.

Delia smiled. "At first she wasn't even willing to talk to me about Dub Robertson and Emily Pierce. But when I told her that I was a successful dime novelist and I was willing to pay her fifty dollars for information, she quickly came around. It was clear that she blames Miss Pierce for everything that happened to Mr. Robertson."

"Yes," Longarm agreed. "But I found it hard to believe that a sixteen-year-old girl, the daughter of a United States marshal, could be such a seductress. Reno is a good-sized town, but even so that kind of behavior could not have been kept a secret."

"I'm not so sure about that," Delia told him. "A clever

girl like Emily would probably have been able to keep a dark side of her life a secret."

"I don't buy it," Longarm said bluntly. "But I've been known to be wrong on occasion. Did Miss Morton have any more information on the young mine owner that Emily was supposedly having an affair with?"

"No, she only knew what Dub Robertson had told her."

Their stagecoach suddenly appeared from around a corner and the owner of the business said, "Looks like you'll be the only passengers today. If I wasn't hauling mail and supplies to Carson City, this trip would be a loss for me with just two passengers."

"Well," Longarm said, "I'm glad you're not losing money."

"You going to return tomorrow?"

"No," Longarm told the man. "We'll be taking the Virginia and Truckee Railroad up to Virginia City after we finish our business in the territorial capital."

"I also own the stage line that runs from Virginia City back here to Reno so we'll see you when you return and I hope you both have an enjoyable trip. It's cool this time of the year and the recent snows mean that there isn't going to be the kind of dust that passengers have to put up with in the summertime. Say, not that it's any of my business, but you two wouldn't be on your honeymoon, would you?"

Before Longarm could answer, Delia slipped her arm through his and smiled sweetly, "No, but thanks for planting the idea."

"Yes, ma'am!"

Longarm helped Delia into the coach and when it left Reno he said, "What the hell did you say a thing like that for?"

"Oh," Delia replied, "I sometimes say things without thinking them through first. And besides, we *do* make a striking couple."

Longarm shook his head and turned his attention to the passing landscape. He wouldn't tell Delia, but she was a deceitful heartbreaker and he'd spent enough time with the dime novelist to know that marrying her would be a terrible mistake. Maybe in ten or fifteen years from now when her looks had began to fade she might turn out to be a good woman, but until then she was going to be hell on men.

"Well," Delia said, as the sun slid behind the Sierras that towered over Nevada's territorial capital, "here we are."

"Yes," Longarm replied, consulting his pocket watch. "I'm sure that most regular businesses are closed by now so we might as well get rooms at the Ormsby House and enjoy a good meal. I can pay a visit to the Mint Jewelry Store owned by a Mr. Teagarden and see if Dub Robertson really was going to buy an engagement ring."

"And while you're doing that, I can visit the mercantile and verify what the woman said about Dub Robertson coming here to buy a sewing machine. I'd say that, by noon, we will know if the seamstress was telling us the truth or not."

"Agreed."

When the stage rolled to a stop, Longarm helped Delia out of the door and pointed up the street. "The Ormsby is the best hotel in town and I'll meet you there in an hour or so."

Delia nodded. "I'm sort of hoping that Miss Morton was lying."

"And why would you hope for that?"

"Because it would mean that the story behind the murders and abduction of a young woman becomes even more mysterious and therefore more enjoyable for my readers."

Longarm didn't quite know what to say to that so he asked and received directions to the Mint Jewelry Store. It was only half a block up the street, and when he entered the establishment a pale and slender but dapper-looking man in his forties put on an engaging smile. The jewelry shop itself was impressive with expensive carpeting and very good original oil paintings. Along each wall display cases were filled with rings, bracelets, watches, and other fine items on display in sparkling glass cases lined with black velvet. In a quick glance, Longarm knew that this was a successful and well-respected business.

"Good afternoon! My name is Elias Teagarden and I'm the owner of this shop. How can I help you today?"

Longarm shook the man's hand while deciding that Mr. Teagarden looked exactly like a jeweler.

"I'm afraid that I'm after information rather than jewelry," he said, showing the man his federal officer's badge and then replacing it in his coat pocket.

"Information?" Teagarden wasn't smiling as broadly now that he had learned that there was no money to be made by Longarm's arrival. "What kind of information?"

"It's pretty straightforward. I need to know if a Mr. Dub Robertson was supposed to buy an engagement ring before he was arrested and then shot to death in a Reno jail cell."

A shadow passed across Teagarden's dark eyes. "As matter of fact, Dub Robertson was supposed to buy an engagement ring for Miss Morton. They couldn't afford anything expensive, but they left a fifty-dollar deposit and I designed a very nice engagement ring with a quarter carat diamond and a sensible but attractive setting. It was a very good value and I was genuinely sorry to hear that the deceased Mr. Robertson was charged with murder and then himself was murdered."

"So Miss Morton and Mr. Robertson did visit you?"

"Of course."

"When?"

"About three weeks ago. I recall that my first impression of the couple was not favorable. The gentleman was poorly dressed and in bad need of a haircut and shave. The lady was . . . well, quite plain. I immediately knew that whatever they wanted to buy here would be inexpensive. But when they told me that they were willing to spend one hundred dollars, I revised my poor opinion. They were not impressive people, but I especially liked Miss Morton and realized that she was a woman of character."

"And what made you change your mind?"

"It was clear that she was religious and she spoke quite proudly of the way that her betrothed was winning the battle against his demons. I could see that Mr. Robertson had led a . . . well, difficult and probably disreputable life and he was trying hard to redeem himself. In the short time that they were here and I drew a few sketches of rings that I could design with a small diamond but which would be very nice . . . I could see that the couple really were in love and quite dependent upon each other."

"How dependent?" Longarm asked.

"Clearly she was trying to get Mr. Robertson to adopt the life and morals of a good Christian and it was just as clear that Miss Morton was not a woman who would have many chances at matrimony. After we agreed on a design and I showed them the diamond I would use for the price they could afford, they left hand in hand and I was touched. So having told you all this, you can understand why I was greatly saddened when I learned the sad outcome."

Over the years Longarm had become a good judge of character, and as the jeweler had related the experience of the couple and their desire for a ring he could see that Teagarden was honest with a big romantic streak . . . a man perfectly suited for his profession.

"I am investigating the murders and the abduction of

Miss Emily Pierce. Do you have anything to add to what you've already told me?"

"I can only say that, if you judged Mr. Robertson by his appearance, you would certainly have thought he was capable of the crime for which he was arrested. But if you took a little time and saw him with Miss Morton, you would change your negative feelings and realize that Mr. Robertson was a man who had made a great many mistakes but could be redeemed. I believe that had he lived to marry Miss Morton, he could have made something of himself."

"Thank you," Longarm said.

"Would you like to see it?"

"What?"

"The ring that should now be on Miss Morton's finger."

"Yes, I would."

The jeweler only had to reach under the counter between them to retrieve the engagement ring with a quarter-carat diamond. He held it up before Longarm's eyes so that it could be admired. The small diamond sparkled and the gold and silver setting in which it had been placed also had two small but pretty red rubies.

"I threw the rubies in at cost," Teagarden admitted. "They are not very big nor are they of the highest quality, but Miss Morton had mentioned that rubies were her birthstone and so I added them as a surprise."

"I'm really sorry that she will never wear that ring."

"Me too, Marshal, and not because of the money. I can sell this little engagement ring for more than one hundred dollars, but somehow, it won't give me much satisfaction or pleasure."

"I understand. Good day, sir."

"Good day, Marshal. I hope you find that missing girl and that she is still alive. And I also hope you find out who really ambushed and murdered Marshal Pierce and his wife on the road between here and Reno."

"You sound as if you are very sure that it wasn't Dub Robertson."

"As sure as I am of death and taxes."

"Thank you," Longarm said as he left with a troubled mind.

"You're most welcome and if you ever decide you might like to sell that fine railroad pocket watch and gold chain, please come to me first and I'll make you a very fair offer."

"I'll keep that in mind."

"So," Longarm said when he and Delia had been seated at the table and the waiter had taken their order. "What did you discover at the mercantile concerning a sewing machine?"

"It was there and the proprietor confirmed that he had ordered it for Miss Morton to be picked up upon arrival. When he learned that Dub Robertson had been arrested for murder and abduction and then was assassinated in a Reno jail cell, he immediately sold the Singer sewing machine to another customer."

"Then everything that Miss Morton told us was the truth."

"Apparently so, poor woman."

"Which leads me to think that Dub Robertson wasn't the man who ambushed Marshal Pierce and his wife and then abducted his daughter."

"So," Delia said, "I guess that we're stuck."

"No," Longarm argued. "We've eliminated the prime suspect, who is deceased, and that means that we just have to dig a bit deeper and discover who else might have committed the crimes."

"What about Emily Pierce? Miss Morton is sure that she had something to do with this crime."

Longarm thought about that for a moment before speaking. "I can find it plausible that Emily was having a secret life unbeknownst to her parents. I can even believe that a sixteen-year-old girl would be having clandestine affairs with older, married men. But I find it impossible to believe that she would go along with having her parents murdered for whatever amount of money they were carrying that day between here and Reno."

"Daughters, like sons, have murdered their parents before."

"I know that but it still doesn't add up for me."

"Then who would have done such a terrible crime and where is Emily?"

"Maybe we'll find those answers up in Virginia City," Longarm replied.

Chapter 15

The Virginia & Truckee Railroad had been constructed to haul heavy loads of ore and supplies between Virginia City, Gold Hill, and Carson City, but it also relied on a steady stream of passengers. It pulled out of the territorial capital and chugged straight east through a sea of sagebrush and rock just north of the Carson River for several miles. Soon, it turned northeast and began to struggle up into the desolate and largely barren mountains dotted with a few scrubby piñon and juniper pines.

"Gawd, this is ugly country!" Delia said as the train moved slowly but steadily higher. "Not a pine tree, river, or stream in sight."

"I told you how hard it must have been for the Forty-Niners who came off the forested western slopes of the Sierra Nevada mountains. But miners will go wherever the ore is to be found. For them, there is always the dream of striking it rich."

"But you said all the gold was found in big pockets deep under Sun Mountain."

"That's almost true. However, small nuggets of gold

were found in dry gullies and streambeds that only fill with water after the torrential spring and summer rains."

"Look at all the mines that were abandoned."

Everywhere a person looked were small piles of tailings where miners working only with picks and shovels and maybe a little dynamite had struggled to burrow into the rocky slopes. Sadly, very few of those tunnels had produced so much as an ounce of gold and it was clear that almost all the scrubby pines had been chopped down by early miners and used either as firewood during the bitterly cold winters or for bracing up the ceilings of the shafts and tunnels.

"What is this town called?"

"Silver City, and then we'll pass up this canyon through Gold Hill before we climb over a ridge and arrive in Virginia City."

"So many businesses shuttered," Delia said, taking notes. "And all those pitiful and falling down shacks! It looks as if hundreds of people once lived here."

"Thousands," Longarm corrected. "I'd guess there are less than five hundred people trying to eke out a living up here now."

"Is Virginia City this deserted?"

"It's been a few years since I've visited the 'Queen of the Comstock Lode' as she was known around the world. But I expect there are hundreds of little shacks and businesses that are deserted. You see, without the mines producing, no one would live up here on this barren mountain. The water, what little there is to be found locally, tastes awful and everything from hay to beer has to be hauled either by mule and wagons or this train and that makes it expensive. When the mines were producing, money wasn't a huge problem, but now . . ."

"Now this is all just a deserted dream," Delia said. "Say,

I like *deserted dream*! It could even be a title for one of my future novels."

"I guess," Longarm said, closing his eyes and tipping his hat over his forehead. "I'm going to get a quick nap before we arrive in Virginia City."

Her hand brushed his thigh. "What's the matter, did I work you too hard last night at the Ormsby Hotel?"

"I'm not complaining but sleep has been a bit hard to come by lately."

"We can sleep in our graves forever," Delia said.

The V&T Railroad, as it was called by locals as well as by historians, rolled into the train station near sundown and about thirty passengers unloaded. There were a half-dozen buggies waiting to deliver the new visitors up the hill to the main part of town along C Street.

"I'd rather walk up that hill," Delia declared, "we've been sitting all day and I could use the exercise."

Longarm shrugged because she was probably right. The climb was steep and given the altitude up on Sun Mountain, he knew they'd quickly be out of breath. A few of the passengers, mostly older and well dressed, elected to pay for a ride up the mountainside, but the miners and workmen along with most others chose to save the fare and walk.

They stayed that night at the Gold Strike Hotel and the next morning they set out to find Maxwell Pennington.

"Where is the sheriff's office?"

"Just down the street a few doors, but he ain't there," a man with a bushy beard, bloodshot eyes, and a dirty flannel shirt replied.

"Where is he?"

"Graveyard. He joined a few others who wore badges here and he was a good man. Can't recall his name, but he had red hair and was cross-eyed. He got gunned down by a gambler named . . . oh, well, it doesn't matter. They hanged the gambler on a hoisting works and instead of burying the bastard, they just tossed his body down an abandoned mine shaft that dropped about eight hundred feet."

"Then who is the law these days?" Longarm asked.

"Ain't any," the man said, picking his nose. "It's every man, woman, and child for themselves anymore."

"What about a newspaper?"

"Oh, we still got one. Old Dan DeQuille is still the editor of the *Territorial Enterprise*. He's gettin' up there in years and used to be a friend of a fella that got pretty famous and now calls himself Mark Twain. You ever hear of him?"

"Sure," Delia said before Longarm could answer. "Who hasn't read *Tom Sawyer* or *Huckleberry Finn*?"

"I ain't," the man confessed. "When Twain worked for the *Territorial Enterprise* he was just a young reporter named Sam Clemens. I guess that handle wasn't good enough for a fella that got famous."

"I guess not," Longarm agreed. "So is editor DeQuille still putting out a paper these days?"

"Oh, sure. He doesn't sell many anymore, but he has a lot of friends in this town. Most likely you'll find him at his desk trying to think up something to write about."

"Thanks for your time, mister," Longarm said.

"Time is all most of us have anymore and mine is runnin' out. Tell Dan I sent you along."

"Will do."

Longarm and Delia had no trouble finding Dan DeQuille and they were shocked by the shabby office and the cadaverous man's frayed clothing. DeQuille was tall with sad eyes and a salt-and-pepper beard. He greeted them cordially and then motioned for them to sit down and rest their feet.

"It's an honor to meet you," Delia gushed. "It must have been quite an experience working with Mark Twain back in Virginia City's heyday."

"It was, but I taught him how to be a good reporter," DeQuille told them. "Me and Sam got along just fine and had a lot of drinks and laughs. We'd try to outdo each other writing up big lies that the locals would fall for. We came up with some real whoppers."

"I'll just bet you did," Delia said.

"Sam got restless here and traveled on to California, of course, and wrote *The Celebrated Jumping Frog of Calaveras County* and after that *Tom Sawyer.* He's immensely talented and when I finish my big epic called *The Big Bonanza*, which will be the definitive work on the Comstock Lode, Sam has promised to help me find a publisher. Maybe then I'll retire and move to San Diego or some other place on the coast where the weather is mild and easier on an old reporter and editor's bones."

"I'm a pretty successful dime novelist," Delia said, giving DeQuille her best smile.

"A dime novelist?"

"That's right! I write under the pen name of Dakota Walker. Maybe you've read a few of my books."

DeQuille shook his head. "Can't say that I have. But I've seen some dime novels and I think they are complete and unimaginative drivel."

Delia's smile melted. "Oh."

"But if you write as pretty as you look, I'm sure that your dime novels are much better than most."

They all realized that DeQuille's last statement was a poor attempt to make Delia feel better about her writing and for a moment, no one had anything to say. Finally, Longarm broke the silence. "Mr. DeQuille."

"Dan. Just call me Dan like everyone else up here does."

"Okay. Dan. We are up here to find a Mr. Maxwell Pennington. Can you help us?"

"Max left Virginia City about five days ago. He took the stagecoach down to Reno and I think I heard that he was headed for his ranch out at Fallon. He spends more and more time there."

"Where is Fallon?" Longarm asked.

"Oh," DeQuille said with a wave of his hand, "it's about seventy or eighty miles east of Reno. I've never been out that way, and from what I've heard, I wouldn't find it appealing."

"And why would he go to Fallon?"

"His father owned a lot of land out there and ran quite a few cattle. But Mr. Pennington died not too long ago and the ranch went to Max. I heard that he inherited about six thousand acres of sage and sand and a good herd of cattle. He supplies beef to some army posts out that way. If he's got water and grass, Max will do a lot better ranching than he did here at the mine the last five or six years."

"Did you ever see him with a blond-haired girl?"

"Sure."

"You did!" Delia whipped out her notepad and pencil. "Could you describe her?"

"Of course," DeQuille said, "but why don't you just go over and see Annie at the Bucket of Blood Saloon where she works?"

The pencil in Delia's hand stopped writing. "You say her name is Annie and she's a saloon girl?"

DeQuille blushed. "Among other things, yes."

Longarm cleared his throat. "I don't think we need to see Annie. Mr. DeQuille, I'm sure you are aware of the ambush of Marshal John Pierce and his wife, Agnes, along with the disappearance of their daughter."

"Of course I am. I even wrote about it in my newspaper and I wasn't above hinting that maybe the girl was still alive although I'm pretty sure that isn't the case."

"Why would you say that?" Delia asked.

"Because, if she is as pretty as described, she'd stand out in this country and someone would have seen and helped her by now. I hate to say this, but she has to be either dead or maybe she was taken down to Mexico."

"That's also my thinking," Longarm added. "Can you tell me about Maxwell Pennington?"

"I could, but first I need to know what business all of this has to do with you and this lady."

Longarm showed DeQuille his badge. "Marshal John Pierce was a fine lawman and his wife a good woman. They didn't deserve to be ambushed and killed. I've been sent from Denver to see if I can get to the bottom of their murders and even to help find their missing daughter."

"I see." DeQuille found his own notepad and pencil. "You don't mind if I take a few notes of my own, do you?"

"I'd rather you didn't until I have a bit more time to investigate."

DeQuille sighed and laid down his pencil. "If I can't take notes, then neither can you, Miss Walker."

"Actually, my real name is Delia Wilson. Dakota Walker is just my pen name."

"Maybe I'd have become famous if I'd have used a pen name like you and Sam," DeQuille mused somewhat ruefully. "Too late now, I suppose."

"Dan," Longarm said, trying to get back to the subject of Maxwell Pennington. "Will you tell me about the young man?"

"He's handsome as anything," DeQuille said. "He's not as tall as you or I, but he's at least six feet with wavy blond hair and blue eyes. The women have always chased Max."

"How long has he lived up here and worked his mine?"

DeQuille thought a moment. "I'd say Max arrived about ten years ago and took the mine over from his father. Back then, it was still producing quite a lot of gold and making Max, his father, and the stockholders wheelbarrows full of money."

"So when did the gold start to run out?"

"About the same time that the Ophir and the other big mines started to go bust . . . seven or eight years ago. Mr. Pennington and Max started fighting as the strain of losing money set in. I've seen it over and over and finally, the father left the Comstock and went out and bought the cattle ranch near Fallon. He would return over the years make sure that Max was still taking out whatever profits could be taken from their mine. But he never stayed more than a day or two and he'd be headed back to Fallon."

"When was the last time you saw the father?" Delia asked.

"Shortly before he went missing and that would be a couple of months ago."

"He went missing?" Longarm asked.

"Yes. He left here and disappeared like smoke."

"Did you actually see him leave?" Delia asked.

"As a matter of fact I did. He and I got along pretty well and we'd had breakfast that morning. I saw him to the stage and we waved good-bye. He was never seen again."

Longarm scowled. "So the father dies and the son inherits not only the mine but the cattle ranch."

"Sure. Max was an only child." DeQuille ran his fingers through his thinning gray hair. "What has Max Pennington got to do with anything?"

Longarm steepled his fingers. "If I tell you, then you have to keep this quiet until I finish my investigation. Miss

Emily Pierce may yet be alive and I'm sure you don't want to jeopardize her chances."

"What chances?"

"I don't know," Longarm confessed. "Listen, Dan, I talked to a woman in Reno who seems honest and reputable. She swears that Maxwell Pennington was seeing Emily Pierce on the sly."

"But the Pierce girl was only sixteen and the daughter of highly respected parents."

"That doesn't matter," Delia interrupted. "Emily Pierce may have fallen in love or been flirting with Pennington. It could have gotten serious."

"Are you actually suggesting that Max might have had something to do with the ambush and abduction?"

"I don't know," Longarm answered. "But the woman that Delia and I both interviewed in Reno said Maxwell Pennington was involved with Emily Pierce and she seemed very credible. Yesterday, we were in Carson City checking out a few details of her story and they were accurate."

DeQuille shook his head. "I think this entire conversation is about as credible as the crap Sam Clemens and I used to write when we couldn't find any *real* stories."

"Be that as it may," Longarm said. "We are here to investigate and even though Max Pennington is not in Virginia City, I'd like to at least see his operation."

"It's called the Empire Mine and you'll find it at the west end of town."

"Is it still being worked?" Delia asked.

"Max has a crabby old fella named Pete who lives and works the mine when he is sober. He likes to sit in a chair and drink whiskey and shoot coyotes and varmints. He calls himself a 'guardian' of the mine so if you go out there and try to get near the Empire, you had better be careful because Pete is the kind that shoots first and asks questions later. He's as loony as a shithouse rat and ornery as a teased snake."

"Thanks for the warning," Longarm said, coming to his feet. "So you never saw any young blond woman other than Annie, who is a saloon girl at the Bucket of Blood?"

"No."

"Then thanks for your time," Longarm said, preparing to leave.

DeQuille stood up quickly. "Will you promise to let me know as soon as you determine what happened to the missing Pierce girl?"

"Do you have a telegraph office here?"

"Of course."

"Then I'll send you a telegram the minute I know anything."

"You may never know anything," DeQuille reasoned. "I just have a bad feeling that Emily Pierce is dead and buried."

"You're probably right."

"Miss Wilson?" DeQuille called as they were on their way out the door.

"Yes?"

"If you use any of this in a dime novel, be sure and spell my name correctly and mention the *Territorial Enterprise*. Might help me get a few more subscribers."

"I'll do that," Delia promised. "And would you like an autographed copy of my latest dime novel?"

"Not really."

Delia swallowed hard and closed the door saying to Longarm, "I'll bet my next dime novel makes one hell of a lot more money than he makes in an entire year as editor of his dying rag."

"Probably so. I think you had better go back to our hotel and wait while I go see the Empire Mine."

"I want to come along."

"Why?"

"Because it will be interesting. And you won't let old Pete shoot us, will you?"

Longarm patted the gun on his hip. "Not if I can possibly help it."

Chapter 16

"That must be it," Longarm said, pointing toward a big hoisting works and tailings pile along with a couple of tin-roofed buildings and cabin or office whose faded paint had peeled off in big patches.

"Yeah, and that old man sitting out in front with a rifle laid across his lap is probably Pete," Delia said. "Looks like he might be taking a nap."

Longarm agreed. Pete was tipped back in a chair resting against the front door of the little building. His boots were propped up on a busted wheelbarrow and his head was tilted back with his hat pulled low over his eyes. Even from a distance they could both hear him snoring.

"The problem is that Pete's guard dog has already seen us and he's pretty damned big and he doesn't look friendly."

"So what do we do?"

Longarm considered their next move. The last thing he wanted to do was to approach Pete and then have the dog suddenly attack. If that happened, he'd probably have to shoot the beast and by then Pete would be shooting at them.

"I think we'd better play this safe and just call out to the man so we don't startle him into doing something stupid."

Before Delia could reply, Longarm cupped his hands around his mouth and yelled, "Hey, Pete! We came to talk with you!"

The dog that looked like a wolf jumped to its feet, hair rising on his shoulders and with its massive head down started in their direction. Longarm could see its bared fangs and he had no doubt at all that the animal's bite would be deep and bloody.

"Delia!" he said, pulling his Colt revolver with one hand and with the other he pushed the woman behind him. "Stay behind me!"

"You're just going to shoot him?"

"If he attacks, then you bet I will."

Longarm cocked back the hammer of the gun and took aim. The dog wasn't running at them, just trotting with its head down and its lips curled. They could hear it growling and snarling. Longarm had been bitten by dogs before and he had no intention of letting this huge dog take a piece out of his arm, leg, or even his throat.

"Pete!" Longarm shouted again. "Don't make me shoot your damned watchdog!"

Pete started awake and almost fell out of his chair. He looked around, momentarily dazed, and saw his dog and the visitors, one with a pistol up and ready to fire.

"Goliath! Come here! Goliath, no!"

But the dog kept coming and just as Longarm was about to fire, Pete yanked up his rife and let off a shot. His bullet struck gravel just behind Goliath and sprayed the dog's ass with flying dirt and rock.

Goliath abruptly changed direction, heading fast for the sagebrush.

Longarm lowered his revolver. "Pete, I need to talk to you!"

"I got nothin' to say to nobody! Git!" To emphasize his point, Pete raised the rifle and pointed it toward Longarm and Delia, levering another shell into the breech.

"The damn fool!" Longarm hissed. He took quick aim and fired. His bullet clipped Pete's hat and sent it flying. Pete shouted and Longarm fired, causing the old man to trip and fall while cussing a blue streak.

Longarm dashed forward, and as Pete made a grab for his rifle, Longarm kicked it aside and grabbed Pete by the throat. "You loco old bastard! I'm a United States marshal and I just came to talk. You could have killed me and the woman!"

Pete coughed out a strangled curse and Longarm slapped him hard across the face. Pete's eyes rolled up in his head and Longarm dragged him to his feet. "Are you crazy or drunk?"

"Let go of me, you big son of a bitch!"

Longarm shook him hard and then let him slump to the ground. "I swear I never met a more foolish old codger."

Pete looked up at him with bloodshot eyes and hissed, "If I was as young as you again, I'd kick your ass from here down to Carson City."

"Never in your best day. Now get up!"

Pete struggled to his feet.

"Where is Maxwell Pennington?" he asked, already knowing the answer but wanting to see if Pete was going to be honest or lie.

"He's off in Fallon! I'm paid to watch this mine, and by gawd, nobody invited you or that woman here."

Longarm signaled for Delia to come and join them. He turned back to Pete. "How come you tried to shoot us when all we wanted to do was talk?"

"Because that's my orders from Mr. Pennington," Pete hissed, touching his bloody lips. "You had no right to slap me that way!"

"You brought it on yourself," Longarm growled. He retrieved the man's rifle and then propped it up against the shack. "Do you live here all the time?"

"Hell yes. What's it to you?"

"I want to know all about your boss."

"Kiss my skinny ass, Marshal!"

"I won't kiss it, you old fart, but I will kick it from one side of this mountain to the other." To get his point across, Longarm drew back his fist and when Pete cringed, he slammed the man up against the shack. "I don't know why you're trying to make this a lot harder than it needs to be."

"What the hell do you want to know about Mr. Pennington?"

"Tell me about the young blond that he was seeing in Reno."

Pete blinked. "How'd you know about her?"

"It's my business to know."

Pete looked past Longarm at Delia. "And how's it supposed to be *that* woman's business?"

"Never you mind her," Longarm snapped. "Just tell me about the blond gal."

Longarm had laid the trap and now he needed to know if Pete was going to step into it. Again, he grabbed Pete by the throat and drew back his hand. "Tell me or I'll bust that nose of yours across your ugly face so hard it will look like a puddle of strawberry jam!"

"All right!" Pete swallowed hard. "Mr. Pennington told me not to tell anyone about what he does or the wimmen he does it with. If you tell him what I said, he'll fire me and nobody will give me a job anymore. I'll gawdamn starve to death and it'll all be your fuckin' fault! Goliath will starve, too! You want the deaths of an old man and a dog on your conscience? Is that what you want, Marshal!"

Longarm didn't release his hold. "You and the dog starving would be way down on the list of bad things I've had to do as a federal lawman. So start talking!"

"Ain't much to tell you about the girl."

"Did he bring her up here to Virginia City and this mine?"

"Just once."

"Do you know her name?"

"Don't know and don't care! But she was young and just as pretty as that woman you're with now."

"When you saw the girl, did Maxwell Pennington use her name?"

"Nope."

"Did she look hurt or scared?"

"No, sir! She was hangin' all over him real lovey-dovey like. I could see that they was lustin' for each other. It was dark when he brought her up and he just stopped here to give me a little food money and then they set off up the street to where Mr. Pennington lives. Big house up on the hill. I never was allowed inside and I don't care about that. But he'd bring women up all the time and take 'em to the big house for a couple of days."

"When did you see this blond girl and was she the last that your boss brought up here?" Delia asked.

Pete glared at Delia. "You sure as shit don't wear a badge, missy! So what the hell do I have to answer your questions for?"

Delia's beautiful face suddenly wasn't beautiful. Her eyes blazed and she looked as if she wanted to bite a big hole in the old watchman's face. "You're scum, Pete! You're the kind of a man that doesn't deserve to breathe and your dog has become just like you."

"Goliath was kicked around as a pup, missy. He got

beat every day by the first man that owned him and when he grow'd big enough, he near tore out the bastard's throat and then he took to the sagebrush. Goliath lived two years as a wild dog catchin' and killin' rabbits and stealing food from the miners until he came around and I started to feed him regularly. Took another two years before I could touch him and he learned to protect me from others."

"Well," Longarm said, voice softening. "I'm glad I didn't have to shoot Goliath. When you sleep you ought to keep him on a chain close at hand. He'd still bark and wake you but he wouldn't go after people. Might be a couple of kids come by and he'd tear them apart."

"Ain't no kids living up on this godforsaken Comstock Lode. Never was but a few."

"All the same," Longarm said. "I can tell that the dog means something to you and you need to make sure that he doesn't kill somebody one of these days."

"If you'd have shot Goliath, I'd have found a way to return the favor," Pete said.

Longarm had met many men like Pete. You couldn't flatter them into being nice and you couldn't reason with them to help you out of a sense of duty or decency. The only thing that men like Pete understood was force and fear.

"When was the last time you saw Mr. Pennington with the young blond girl?"

"About ten days or two weeks ago."

"And did you ever see the girl since?" Delia asked.

"Nope." Pete's eyes shifted up and down Delia's body. "You're the kind of woman that would have caught Mr. Pennington's eye. He'd have sweet-talked you into his bed in no time at all."

Delia's cheeks flushed and she turned her back to them.

Pete winked at Longarm. "You got a looker there, Marshal. Bet she's a wildcat on a rug or a thin mattress."

Longarm shook his head, not knowing whether to put his fist in the old man's leering face or just to turn his back as Delia had done and walk away. "Where is this big house that your boss owns?"

He pointed. "Up there at the top of the hill. Got a wrought-iron fence around it painted black. You'll see the Pennington name fixed to the gate." Pete licked his bloody lips. "But like I told you, Marshal, Mr. Pennington ain't here now. Probably humpin' that pretty yeller-haired girl on a steer or buffalo hide in front of his Fallon fireplace. Oh, yeah, and he'll be makin' her buck and squeal!"

Longarm suddenly couldn't stand to be near this dirty, disgusting old man. He supposed that Pete's only redeeming value was that he had saved the wolf-dog Goliath. They made a real good pair.

"You didn't ask me nothin' about this Empire Mine!" Pete called as Longarm and Delia started to leave.

Longarm turned. "Does the hoisting works and that steam engine still work?"

"Sure do! I go down now and then huntin' for gold. Ain't found much lately. But someday I will and then me and Goliath gonna leave this stinkin' country."

Longarm pivoted around and saw that Goliath had rejoined his master by the shack. He studied the pair for a moment, then yelled, "That wolf dog deserves a second chance at life . . . but you sure as hell don't!"

"Go sod yourself, you big, overgrown son of a bitch! And then sod that pretty bitch of a woman!"

"I think I'll go back and kill him with my bare hands," Delia said in a voice that trembled with rage.

And she actually did start back, but Longarm grabbed her around the waist and turned her away. "There is nothing but anger, hatred, and evil back at that mine. The real question is this . . . who was the pretty blond girl that he said his boss brought by that night? Could it have been Miss Emily Pierce?"

"I'm sure it must have been."

"Maybe, but maybe not. It's clear that Maxwell Pennington is a womanizer, and he if he's as handsome as the editor told us, he'll have had a lot of young women and some of them would have been blonds."

"You don't think that the one that old man was talking about was Emily Pierce?"

"I just don't know."

"So do we leave for Fallon tomorrow?"

"I'd say that we take a look inside the Pennington house first, and then we decide our next move."

Delia took his arm. "Do you think that . . . that Emily might have been there and even have died at Pennington's house up on that hill?"

"It's a possibility," Longarm replied. "And if so, I'll smell the death and we ought to find evidence of blood."

Delia looked up at him. "If you don't mind, I think I'll go back to the hotel, get a bottle, and go take a hot bath. That old man back there . . . the way he talked and his expression when he spoke of the women . . . well, I need to get drunk and take a bath . . . if I don't throw up first."

"I'll take you by the hotel and then I'll wait until dark and get inside the Pennington house. I'll most likely be back in time to take you to a late dinner."

"Don't hurry because I don't think I could keep any food down this evening."

Longarm smiled grimly. "Maybe you're not quite as hard and callous inside as I thought."

"Keep thinking that, Custis, and I'll get to you yet."

Longarm barked a hollow laugh as they walked back into the heart of Virginia City.

Chapter 17

Longarm arrived at the Pennington house about seven
o'clock that evening after the winter sun had set and everything was clothed in darkness. He studied the two-story
Victorian only a moment and then opened the gate and
walked quickly up to the front porch. He knocked and
when there was no answer just as he'd expected, Longarm
moved around the house looking for an easy entry. He
found it in the back where a door to the kitchen had a latch
and lock. Using a rusty shovel, it took him only a few minutes to pry the latch away and then he moved inside.

"Anyone home!"

He didn't expect an answer and didn't get one, but it
didn't hurt to make certain that the house was empty. After
a few minutes of fumbling around in the dark, Longarm
found a kerosene lantern and moments later he was moving room by room through the house, looking for evidence
of murder in the form of bloodstains or bullet holes. It took
less than five minutes to cover the downstairs carefully
enough to know that whoever had last been in the house
had liked their liquor. There were whiskey and wine bot-

tles stacked up on the kitchen table and remains of old, moldy meals along with dirty dishes.

"Pigsty," Longarm said to himself as he headed for the upstairs bedrooms.

The second room that he entered was the spacious master bedroom with a large window that offered a view of the city lights just down the hill. The bed was enormous and unmade. Longarm slowed his search, looking very carefully at the bedsheets and pillows. He saw lipstick and a woman's rouge on the pillowcases and there was a big mirror suspended on velvet cords from the ceiling directly over the bed. Piled on the floor in a corner near the bed were expensive women's nightgowns and underwear; most interesting because they were of all different sizes. There was an ashtray spilling over with cigar butts, all Cuban. On the walls were some very good nudes including one with a grinning man with a huge erection standing next to a smiling girl spread-eagled on a bed who looked to be about fourteen. The girl was blond and buxom.

"Delia would have appreciated this seducer's lair," he said with a trace of amusement.

On the other side of the bed were a man's rumpled clothes and a bathrobe with Oriental designs that still reeked of cologne. Two empty bottles of champagne lay on a Persian carpet and in the closet were a dozen silk shirts and eight pairs of shoes and boots. Everything was in disarray and the room gave Longarm the impression that it had been hastily vacated. Longarm also found a couple of opium pipes, which told him even more.

He bent down and studied the Persian carpet, finding a few strands of long blond hair but no bloodstains. What it looked like, Longarm decided, was a bedroom you would expect to find in a very expensive New Orleans whorehouse.

Longarm scowled and held the lamp up overhead taking one last look around and trying to gauge Maxwell Pennington. It wasn't hard to deduct that the man was something of a pig and a wastrel . . . someone drawn to debauchery and sexual orgy.

A pure hedonist.

Longarm could find nothing else of interest or evidence of foul play. He frowned with disappointment and headed for two more bedrooms across the hall. One of them was large and neat. The walls were filled with bookshelves stocked with tomes mostly relating to American and English history. A heavy leather chair looked well used, and there were notes on a desk table along with writing materials. Longarm set his lamp down on the table, took a seat and thumbed rapidly through the papers, quickly learning that they were banking, mining, and assay reports. And although he was unfamiliar with such reports, it was easy enough to see that the accounts painted a very bleak financial picture for the Empire Mine.

Two letters were from creditors demanding payment and threatening lawsuits if money was not immediately forthcoming.

Longarm surveyed the room, noting the oil paintings of well-recognized American landscapes, the neatly made bed, the lack of empty liquor bottles or overflowing ashtrays. This room could not have been more different from the one across the hall and, if he had to guess, it had belonged to the elder and missing Mr. Pennington.

Longarm was about to leave when something on the floor caught his eye. It was the rug and it was pushed up against a wall so that it was slightly bowed. Normally, such a small thing would not have caught his attention, but the rest of the bedroom was so orderly that it seemed odd.

"Hmmm," he mused aloud, staring at the round rug,

which was roughly six feet in diameter, and then on impulse tugging at it. It seemed to be cemented to the floor, and he had to put the lantern down and really put his back to it to tear the rug up from the floor. He tossed it aside and then picked up the lantern for a closer look.

"Oh, my," he said, taking in a sharp breath, because under the rug and no doubt causing it to feel pasted to the floor was a very large, crusted, and blackened pool of blood.

"Murder," he said to himself as he found his pocket-knife, unfolded the longest blade, and began to scrape at the blood. "Someone was murdered right here in this room and the rug was either pulled over to conceal the stain, or else dragged in from another part of the house. Not that it matters."

Moments later, he was digging a misshapen lead bullet out of the hardwood floor. "Forty-five caliber."

Longarm refolded his knife and dropped it along with the bullet into his pocket, and then he looked around for a few more minutes finding nothing.

"So where is the body?" he asked, before briefly checking the last bedroom and finding nothing.

Downstairs, he walked around for a few moments lost in thought and then he remembered that rusty shovel that he'd used to pry off the back door latch. He also remembered he had seen a miner's pick.

Longarm hurried outside and searched the backyard, looking for the sign of a recent burial. It didn't take him long to see where the hard, rocky ground had been overturned as evidenced by clods. Longarm toed the dirt and thought it felt spongy and loose, unlike the surrounding yard dirt.

He studied the ground and considered attacking it with the rusty pick or shovel and immediately rejected the idea. In the dark with only the lantern, he might overlook or disturb something important. Better, much better to wait until tomorrow and then return with at least one or two observers.

Dan DeQuille immediately came to mind along with Delia.

"Yes," he said, "and besides, I'm hungry and Delia is waiting. Tomorrow we will find out what is buried in the Pennington backyard."

Would it be poor, foolish Miss Emily Pierce, or would it be the senior Mr. Pennington? Or maybe it would be one of the Virginia City ladies of the night that made had the fatal mistake of coming to party with Maxwell Pennington before being brutalized, perhaps even sodomized, cruelly tortured, and then sadistically murdered.

Chapter 18

"So," Delia said, wringing her hands together with ill-concealed excitement. "It looks like we are going to find the body of either Emily or the senior Mr. Pennington."

"It could be something or someone else," Longarm told her. "We'll just have to wait and see. But I want Dan DeQuille to be there with us when we dig so that we have a reputable witness."

"To murder."

"I wish it were that simple."

"What do you mean?"

Longarm paused. "I mean that even if it *is* a body and we can identify it as belonging to Emily or the senior Mr. Pennington, it's going to be a difficult to prove that the person was murdered by Max Pennington."

"But you just showed me the bullet and told me that a rug had been . . ."

"I know," Longarm said. "But let's suppose it is the father. And let's assume that Maxwell Pennington isn't stupid. So if you or I were Maxwell, would it really be that hard to claim that his father or the girl had perhaps gotten a hold of a gun and a bottle and gone crazy? Crazy enough to have committed suicide?"

Delia's eyes widened. "What?"

"Suicide or an accident," Longarm told Delia. "That's what any reasonably intelligent lawyer defending Maxwell Pennington would claim. And how in the world could that be disproved?"

"But why would a beautiful girl or a decent, respected man like Mr. Pennington shoot themselves?"

"Let's just suppose I am the lawyer defending charges against the younger Mr. Pennington. I'd most likely say that the girl was lovesick and when Maxwell made it clear that he was just using her for sex and was going to cast her aside, she shot herself."

"Oh, come on!"

"And if we exhume a corpse and can actually prove it is the elder Pennington, a defense attorney would likely claim that the man had committed suicide because of impending financial ruin and humiliation. It happens, Delia. And that would be enough to get Maxwell off free and clear."

Delia threw up her hands. "I can't believe that you're telling me this."

"I am because I've seen it happen time and time again. A man with money hires a good defense attorney and then spins a tale that can't be proven or disproven. Because of the doubt, a jury has no choice but to come to a verdict of not guilty."

"But . . . but we both know that Maxwell Pennington is a vile womanizer and probably has been cheating his father on the mine income for years."

"Yes, but being a womanizer isn't the same as a murderer nor is cheating one's father out of money."

Delia's fists balled in frustration. "Custis, you and I both know that Maxwell Pennington is behind the disappearance of both Emily and his father."

"We *suspect* he is, but we aren't completely certain."

"Then how—"

"I don't know," Longarm interrupted. "But what I do know is that we have to go to Fallon and meet the man and then figure out some way to get evidence of murder . . . one murder, preferably two."

"I won't sleep tonight thinking about what we might dig up tomorrow in that backyard."

"Do your best, Delia."

"I'm going to take some notes after we eat. Any problem with that?"

"None at all," Longarm replied. "What I do know is that tomorrow . . . unless we dig up a dog or something completely unexpected . . . we are going to give Mr. DeQuille one of the best stories he's had in years."

Longarm slept well that night but Delia had not. There were dark circles under her eyes and she was out of sorts. "I swear I don't know how you can sleep so soundly when there is so much on the line today."

"Why worry about it?" Longarm asked. "Either we find a body or we don't. And like I said last evening, even if we can identify them, that doesn't offer proof that Max Pennington will be convicted of murder."

Delia turned away from their upstairs hotel room window. "I'm ready to go and find Dan DeQuille."

"It's only seven o'clock. I'm sure he isn't in his office yet."

"Well, can't we find out where the man lives and hurry this along!"

"Take it easy, Delia. Let's have a good breakfast and then we'll go find the editor."

Delia was ready to go and when they went downstairs, the surly old guard from the Empire Mine was sitting in the lobby with his rifle resting across his knees.

"Uh-oh," Delia said. "I think we've got a problem."

"Stay back and let me handle this," Longarm ordered.

Pete stood up and it was clear by the look on his face that he was furious. "I hear that you were snoopin' around the Pennington house last night."

"Who told you that?"

"It's a small town and there aren't many secrets."

"All right," Longarm said, "I was at the house last evening. I'm a United States federal marshal and I don't have to explain my actions to you."

Pete's mouth twisted and he spat, "Mr. Pennington pays me not only to watch over his mine, but also his house when he's gone. Did you break into it?"

"Yes, I did."

Pete swore and tried to yank his rifle up, but Longarm was ready and drove a wicked uppercut into the man's stomach. Pete folded up and collapsed to his knees, sucking for air. Longarm grabbed the man's rifle and tossed it aside.

"Get up!" Longarm commanded, grabbing Pete by the collar and jerking him to his feet.

"I'll get you for that," Pete managed to wheeze.

Longarm propelled the man over to a corner away from Delia and two other gawking guests. "Pete," he said in a low voice, "I found a lot of blood in an upstairs bedroom covered by a rug. And in the backyard there's fresh evidence of a grave. You are coming with me to the house this morning and if I find a body or even suspect that you've had anything to do with murder, I'll take you down to Reno and put you in their jail. You'll be charged as an accomplice to murder . . . and I suspect you were paid to do the job all by yourself."

"What!" Pete's jaw dropped. "I ain't ever killed someone except twice when it was in self-defense."

"You can tell that to a judge and jury. Now where can I find the editor of the *Territorial Enterprise*, Dan DeQuille?"

"He lives alone in a room behind the newspaper office. What has he got to do with anything?"

"He's going to be a witness and get a story . . . one way or the other." Longarm collected Pete's rifle and motioned for Delia to join them. "Pete is coming along with us this morning. In fact, he's going to do the digging."

"The hell you say!"

Longarm drew back his fist. "You'll dig, and you better hope that we don't find a body or you're under arrest."

"I didn't kill anyone!"

"If we find a body, you can tell that to a Reno judge."

Forty-five minutes later, Longarm, Delia, DeQuille, and Pete stood in grim anticipation behind the Pennington house.

"Right there," Longarm said, pointing. "Start digging, Pete."

DeQuille said, "I'd like to go upstairs and see that pool of dried blood."

"Go ahead," Longarm told the man. "Delia, you came with me wanting some 'real' crime to inject into your dime novels. Maybe you'd like to accompany Mr. DeQuille for a few minutes?"

She gave him a quick, emphatic shake of her head. "No. I can imagine what a big pool of dried blood looks like."

"It also has a smell," Longarm informed her. "But you'd have to put your nose closer to it because it isn't fresh."

Delia blanched and looked like she was going to get sick.

"It's one thing to spin a yarn with a lot of blood and

guts being spilled," Longarm said, intent on driving home a point to the intrusive dime novelist, "but quite another to actually see the real thing."

"I . . . I never had a real stomach for seeing death," Delia admitted. "And if there's a decaying body under this backyard, I don't even want to be near it."

"Maybe you should go back to the hotel and wait."

"I'll wait off a ways," she decided.

"Pete, start digging."

The man grabbed the shovel that Longarm had used the night before to pry off the latch to the back door. "I ain't got anything to do with no murders," he declared.

"Just dig!" Longarm ordered.

In less than five minutes, they uncovered a corpse and it was easy to see that it belonged to a man. Longarm grabbed the corpse by the ankles and with Pete's help, they pulled it out of the shallow grave. It looked even worse than it smelled and Delia rushed down the hill toward town, a handkerchief pressed to her face.

"Mr. DeQuille, you can see the suit and tie and there is an expensive ring on the finger. Is this the body of Mr. Pennington?"

"Yes," DeQuille said quietly. "There's no doubt about that."

Longarm took a deep breath and quickly examined the decaying corpse. "The back of his head was smashed in so we know for certain that he was murdered."

"It must have been Maxwell," DeQuille said quietly. "He and his father were very much at odds for the last few years."

Longarm quickly searched the man's pockets. It was a grisly task but one that had to be done. He found a wallet and some change along with a pocketknife and little else.

"Well, Pete," Longarm said, quickly finishing this work, "as of right now you are a suspect in the murder of Mr. Pennington."

"Why me? I had nothing to gain by his death!"

"I'm not so sure of that," Longarm said, walking away with the others following. "You might have been working in cahoots with Maxwell because it's clear that you were being paid by the son and not the father. At the very least, you might have been the one who helped Maxwell bury his father."

"And why would you think that?" DeQuille asked, notepad out and scribbling furiously.

"Because this ground is as hard as a rock. It would have required a great deal of effort to dig . . . to almost chisel . . . that grave. I have never met Maxwell but from what I've heard and seen in the house he doesn't seem like the kind of a man who would go to that much hard physical effort. It would have caused blisters on the palms of his hands and a great deal of exertion."

"That's a good conclusion," DeQuille mused. "Even trying to plant a small rosebush in this flinty ground is a major undertaking."

"So," Longarm said, turning back to Pete, "that means that Maxwell Pennington had to have had some muscle and you are the prime suspect."

Pete backed up against the house, eyes flicking from Longarm to DeQuille and then down to the corpse. Suddenly, he screamed an oath and came at Longarm with the shovel.

Longarm wore his Colt on his left hip, butt forward, and his hand shot to the weapon and yanked it free when Pete was almost on top of him. He fired and the shovel sliced down and hit him on the left shoulder. The pain was instant and intense, but Longarm fired once more and Pete went down twitching, one leg dropping into the newly unearthed grave.

"You helped Maxwell Pennington bury his father!" Longarm shouted at the dying man. "Go out with a clear conscience, damn you! Admit that it was you or Maxwell who killed that man!"

Pete's eyes were glazing over and there was a bloody froth on his lips. They moved and Longarm bent close to hear the man's last words of confession.

"Fuck . . . *you*!"

The pencil and notebook slipped from DeQuille's hand and fell to the earth. He shook his head and studied the two bodies. "This is going to be a great story, but one I'd rather not have written. Mr. Pennington was a good and decent man and he sure didn't need to die like that and be buried in a shallow hole in the ground."

"I know he was your friend and I'm sorry."

DeQuille sighed. "I guess the thing to do next is for us to walk back to town and find our only remaining undertaker. I really don't have the funds to give Mr. Pennington the burial he deserves and as for Pete . . ."

"The ring," Longarm said, removing a ring from Pennington's finger. "It's gold with a large diamond. I'm surprised that Maxwell didn't take it before he buried his father. I guess he decided that it would link him to the murder and it was a risk he couldn't afford to take. Use it and whatever money is in the wallet I retrieved along with the value of the ring to pay for an impressive funeral."

DeQuille agreed. "I'll do that and if there is money left over, I'll give it to a worthy charity. But I'm curious about something."

"What?"

"How can you disprove that old Pete didn't murder

Mr. Pennington and bury him with the same shovel you made him use to unearth the poor man?"

"I can't," Longarm confessed. "But I'm going to Fallon and I'll find Maxwell and play the best hand I can think of in order to get a full confession."

"You'll run a bluff," DeQuille guessed.

"Yes," Longarm admitted. "Because it's really all I can do."

"I don't think Maxwell will bluff. He's not one to scare or panic and he's smart."

"Then there is always torture," Longarm said quietly. "If he is guilty of killing the entire Pierce family and then his own father, you can bet your bottom dollar I'm not going to let him get away with it."

"I'm never going to tell anyone what you just said about torture," DeQuille said quietly. "But in this case, justice must be served and I wouldn't hold it against you to use whatever force was necessary."

DeQuille looked at Pete's body. "Did he really say what I think he said with his dying breath?"

"Yes. Pete was a hard and dangerous man. He said he'd never killed anyone except in self-defense, but I don't believe that even for a moment."

"I wonder if I can find someone to take care of Goliath," DeQuille mused. "Despite his size and ferocity, I think he's a very noble dog."

"That wolf dog can take care of himself."

"Goliath likes and trusts me. I may take him in myself. I think, in time, he could be a good and loyal companion."

"Then you should do that," Longarm agreed, the stench really getting to him now. "Let's go find the undertaker. I sure don't envy him this job."

Chapter 19

Two days later Longarm and Delia were being bounced around by a badly potholed road while seated in a stage-coach nearing Fallon, Nevada. The countryside was not as green as Longarm had expected, but he did see plenty of cattle grazing on the short grass and not a small number of sheep.

"This country reminds me of Elko . . . dry and bleak," Delia glumly observed. "If Maxwell Pennington inherited a big ranch out here in this poor country, I can't imagine him raising any sizable number of cattle."

"Me, neither," Longarm agreed. "But this is good sheep country from the size and number of flocks we've seen on these sagebrush hills and valleys."

The day was cold and the wind was blowing hard. Long-arm figured that the driver must be miserable up on top but at least the recent snowfall had been just enough to keep the dust down. "Delia?"

"Yes?"

"I think you should remain in town until I confront Maxwell Pennington out at his ranch."

"Are you serious?"

"Yes."

"Please," Delia begged, "don't leave me sitting in some hotel room waiting and wondering what in the world you are up to at the Pennington's ranch. Why, it's not completely inconceivable that Emily Pierce might even be hiding out there."

"No, it's not," Longarm agreed. "But if she is, then it will be pretty clear that she had a role in the murders of not only her parents . . . but also of the senior Mr. Pennington."

"You don't think that's possible, do you?"

"Until I face Maxwell and confront him with the murder and death of his father, I have no way of knowing what happened."

"But, Custis, a beautiful, well-raised young woman of sixteen isn't likely to have been a part in such terrible crimes."

"I hope not, but it's possible."

"I just have to go with you to the ranch."

"What if Pennington has men and they all try to kill us?" Longarm asked. "Because that is also a possibility."

Delia's expression grew somber. "Then we'd have to kill them first."

"There might be quite a few men with Maxwell. The odds would not be in our favor."

"But you're a United States marshal, surely they wouldn't . . ."

"Emily's father was a United States marshal and he was murdered, so why do you think they wouldn't dare do the same to you and me?"

Delia considered the question for several moments then answered, "Maybe there is a sheriff in Fallon and we can get him to come along with us."

"I've already decided that would be a good idea." Longarm waved at a cowboy who was driving a few cattle north-ward. "But there is something to consider if I involve the local lawmen."

"What?"

"In smaller towns like Fallon the sheriff is usually an elected official. To get elected and reelected takes money and support from the powerful and wealthy people in the community. That means that the sheriff is beholden to them and is most likely not at all interested in seeing them be arrested . . . especially by a federal officer of the law."

"Are you saying that if we ask the local sheriff to go with us to the ranch he might actually turn out to be some-one that will side with Maxwell Pennington against *us*?"

"That's exactly what I'm saying," Longarm told her. "It's happened to me often enough in the past that I try to avoid getting into that kind of a situation. In the worst case, it could prove to be a fatal mistake."

"So are you or aren't you going to visit Fallon's sheriff?"

"I'm going to visit him on some kind of pretext other than trying to determine if Maxwell is a murderer and if Emily Pierce is still alive."

"A pretext, huh?"

"Yes."

"You mean a lie of some kind so that the man has no idea of why we are here."

"That's right."

Delia smiled. "All right, let me come up with your pre-text. After all, I'm the imaginative dime novelist."

"Okay, before we reach town, give me a great story that a sheriff will believe."

"Hmmm," Delia mused. "Let's tell the man that we are honeymooning and that Maxwell Pennington is an old friend that invited us to visit him and stay awhile at his ranch."

"Not bad."

"It's pretty good, actually."

"Unless the sheriff insists on taking us out to the Pennington ranch."

"In that case, you'll have to come up with a reason why we want to go out there alone."

Longarm considered the matter. "I'll tell the sheriff that we want to surprise Maxwell. That should do it."

"Maybe."

Longarm had to grin. "So I saw you writing furiously yesterday and I was wondering how much of all this is going into your next novel. Remember your promise to change all the names, dates, and places."

"I don't use dates and I'm always vague on places . . . mostly because I haven't seen them and therefore can't describe them."

"I understand."

"But you can bet that many of my future dime novels will be set in places that we have been visiting since we left Denver together . . . the Comstock Lode being one of them."

"Don't get poor Dan DeQuille in trouble."

"I wouldn't dream of it."

"Or me."

Delia snorted a laugh and gave him a kiss on the cheek. "Custis, you *are* trouble! And by the way, how is your shoulder feeling where Pete hit you with that shovel?"

"It's bruised and sore, but not too bad. If he'd have hit me in the head, it would have killed me."

"You've got a hard head so I doubt that you would have suffered all that much."

"And you've got a big head, Delia."

"But also a pretty one."

"True."

"That must be Fallon," Delia said, leaning close to the window and pointing up ahead. "From what I can see, it's about the same size and appearance as Elko."

"Both are mainly cattle towns so that shouldn't come as any surprise."

Longarm rolled his shoulders and gritted his teeth. The blow that Pete had delivered on the top of his left shoulder was painful but he could still move his arm well enough. He just hoped that Fallon's sheriff was an honest man and would help them discover the truth about the murderers. And if they were very lucky and this was to have any kind of a good ending, Emily would be at the Pennington ranch and she would have had no earthly idea that her handsome lover was the cold-blooded killer of her parents.

Unlikely, Longarm thought as they grew nearer to Fallon, *very, very unlikely.*

Chapter 20

"Sheriff Hopper's office is just up the street. You can't miss it," a cowboy told them in front of the Dusty Trail Saloon. "But at this time of the day, his office door is likely locked."

"It's one o'clock in the afternoon," Delia said. "Why . . ."

"Sheriff Hopper likes to take a little nap after his noon meal. He says that because he has to go out at night sometimes when there's trouble, he deserves a nap."

"The hell with that," Longarm snapped. "But thanks for the information."

"You'd better have something important to say if you wake him up or he'll be madder'n an old grizzly bear comin' out of his hibernation."

"We all have our trials," Longarm said, taking Delia's arm and leading her up the street. Somehow, word must have spread that a beautiful new woman had just arrived in town because men actually came out of their shops to stare.

"You do attract a crowd, Delia."

"I know. I have for years and I like it."

"I expect so." They stopped in front of the sheriff's office and Longarm tried the doorknob. "Locked."

He began to pound on the door hard enough to cause it to shake, and then they both heard an angry shout from inside. "Who the hell is it at this hour!"

Longarm didn't answer but kept pounding.

"We're sure not getting off on the right foot here," Delia offered. "He's going to be uncooperative."

"Good. That means that he'll likely be mad enough to tell us the truth about how he feels toward Maxwell Pennington."

"Gawdamnit!" Hopper shouted. "Stop hammering on my damned door!"

"Then open the damned thing," Longarm yelled, "before I kick it in."

Hopper unlocked the door and tore it open. He was a big man with three double chins and very little hair on his head other than a long, tobacco-stained mustache. "Who the hell are you?"

"We're looking for the Pennington ranch," Longarm replied.

"Well, do you think the fuckin' ranch is in my office!" Suddenly, the sheriff realized Delia was standing right behind Longarm. "Oh, sorry, ma'am."

"That's all right. Can we come inside for a minute?"

Sheriff Hopper wasn't wearing any shoes or boots, just a pair of socks with holes in them and he reeked of tobacco and smoke. Even in his socks he was almost as tall as Longarm and fifty pounds heavier. His belt was unbuckled probably to give some comfort to a large beer belly. To Longarm's way of thinking, he was a damn sorry-looking sheriff.

"What are you all gawkin' at!" Hopper shouted at some cowboys across the street that'd gathered to watch Delia and now were grinning at this new and unexpected turn of events. "Go on and get about your business!"

The cowboys didn't budge and Hopper's face grew red with anger. He was about to yell something else at them when Longarm firmly pushed him back into his office and closed the door so they could speak in private.

"Have a seat if you can find one," Hopper grumbled. "Couldn't this business about the Pennington place wait until after my nap? I had to roust a couple of boys from the Rafter Bar Ranch last night and I'm running short of my badly needed rest."

"We're sorry to bother you, Sheriff Hopper," Delia said in her sweetest voice. "We've heard how hard you work for this town."

"You have?"

"That's right."

"Well, that's nice to hear for a change," Hopper said, brightening. "I been sheriff of this town for eight years and it seems like eighty. They don't pay me enough to have any deputies and I only get fifty cents a day for prisoner's food and my own when I'm stayin' here overnight. I'm not young anymore and I got no pension or savings. My wife ran out on me twelve years ago and she married a railroad engineer. They have a hell of a nice home in Reno and my kids are grown and never come to see me. Life has been hard and I can only see it get harder as my health declines."

"I'm sorry for your troubles," Delia said as if she really meant it. "And also sorry for the interruption. But we just wanted to pay you a visit."

"Why?"

"Because my father was a sheriff in a little Wyoming town even smaller than this one and he always told me that when I visited a new town to pay my respects to the underpaid lawman in charge. He said it was the right and decent thing to do."

Hopper plopped into an office chair. He scratched his belly and yawned. "Well, if your father was a lawman in a small town, then he understood how poorly paid and appreciated we are. So what brings you here wanting to visit Max Pennington?"

"He was a good friend of mine," Longarm said. "We were in the mining business up in Virginia City."

"That went to hell in a handbasket. Did you lose your ass by hanging on too long there like the Pennington men?"

"I sold out six years ago," Longarm said. "Did pretty well."

Hopper studied Longarm for a moment and said, "It appears you have done well."

"We are honeymooning," Delia said, feigning a blush. "We've only been married two weeks."

"Well, I'll be. And why in blazes did you come here instead of goin' someplace nice?"

"Like I said, Maxwell invited us and we thought it would be interesting to come and visit him at his ranch."

"It ain't been his for long," the sheriff told them. "Maxwell's father went missing just a short while back. Probably murdered and tossed down one of those abandoned Comstock mines. They're so deep a body would never be found there."

"How tragic!" Delia cried, hand fluttering to her mouth. "So no one has ever found the poor man?"

"No. Maxwell put out a reward but it was never collected. The authorities investigated but found nothing. Mr. Pennington was pretty well regarded here in Fallon and since he loved his ranch and spent most of his days here we had a funeral for him. It was damned impressive if I do say so myself. Black pair of matching horses, shiny black hearse, flowers, and lots of tears and fine words shed and spoken at his gravesite. Did you know the man?"

"Afraid not," Longarm said.

"Too bad. He was real generous with this town and he helped me get elected. I owed him like most everyone around did."

"What about Max?" Longarm asked. "Is he pretty popular as well?"

"Sure. But Max ain't nothing like the old man. He's pretty quick with his temper and I've had to arrest him a few times for fighting and raising hell. But he has a good heart and the women flock to him like bees to honey."

"Yes," Delia said, "I know all about that!"

Longarm blinked with surprise but before he could say a word, Delia continued. "Maxwell and I had our little . . . uh, fling some time back."

Hopper leered and laughed. "Yeah, I can picture that. No offense, sir, but it just seems easy to imagine your wife and Max had some . . . some history."

Longarm acted offended by scowling. "Maybe we ought to just let you go back to taking a nap. I told Delia that we could come by on our way out of town just as easy as now."

"Aw, don't worry about it. Besides, Max has his hands full right now with a mighty pretty young thing."

"He does?"

"Yep," Hopper said, making no attempt to hide a smile. "She's younger than most he's brought here and prettier than a sunflower in springtime. Yellow hair and a tiny waist with a big bosom. She's a dandy, all right."

"Is she at the ranch now?"

"Far as I know. But she never comes to town. We saw her when she arrived with Max in a buggy and they bought some ranch supplies and then she never came back." Hopper winked. "I expect he's got her tied to the bedposts . . . I know if I had her that's what I'd do."

"My oh my!" Delia exclaimed. "It sounds as if Max hasn't changed at all since I knew him."

Hopper's jaw sagged and he grunted, "Did he tie you to his bedposts?"

Delia tittered and looked away. "Oh, we don't tell our most naughty of little secrets, do we?"

"Hellfire! If you tell me yours, then I'll tell you mine!"

Longarm went over and grabbed Delia's hand and pulled her toward the door. "Give us directions."

"Two miles north out of town you'll see where the road forks by an old cottonwood tree. Take the right fork and you'll soon come to the ranch gate. Whole damn place is fenced with barbed wire and the senior Mr. Pennington liked to keep the gate locked but then men started cutting the wire so he threw away the padlock. You can ride right in and you'll see the Pennington house up in a stand of big cottonwoods. Nice place. Max really inherited a fine herd of cattle and good water. Even with his wild ways he's bound to make a profit there . . . if that pretty young thing with the golden hair don't give him heart failure in his bed."

"Thanks," Longarm said, closing the door and leading Delia down the street. "So we found out quite a lot."

Delia stopped abruptly and turned her face up to him. "Custis, do you think it's her? Do you think it's Emily Pierce?"

"More than likely."

"And do you think she's there because she wants to be with Maxwell . . . or is she being held hostage by the man?"

"Only one way to find out and that's to go out to the ranch and see."

"I hope she's a hostage, a sex slave for him."

"Why?"

"Because," Delia said, "if she isn't it must mean that she helped Maxwell Pennington kill her own parents!"

"More than likely," Longarm repeated with a dark scowl on his handsome face.

"Do you think that he might really . . . really tie her to his bedposts?"

"It wouldn't be the first time it has happened or the last."

"I'm going to use all of this in my next dime novel! It will turn my editor's hair gray but it will sell a million copies!"

Longarm's expression softened. "Just go ahead and do that but remember that . . ."

"I know. Change all the names and places." Delia brightened. "When we get there I just have to sneak into the man's bedroom and see if there are manacles or straps attached to his bedposts! I can't wait to find that out."

"Delia," Longarm said, "you are hopeless."

"I know but I've never tried to convince you otherwise." She looked up at him. "And besides, you're no saint, either. In fact, in the bedroom you can be a real devil."

"I'll take that as a compliment," Longarm replied, grinning.

"So where are we going now?"

"We need to rent a couple of saddle horses."

"Can't we rent a buggy? I don't how to ride a horse."

"You don't?"

"No. I don't even like them."

"All right, you've got a lot more money than I do so you rent the horse buggy."

"With pleasure."

They spied a livery up the street and their pace quickened. "Custis?"

"Yeah?"

"You forgot to ask if there are a lot of tough men on the ranch payroll."

"There will be," Longarm said, glancing around. "I can size up the territory as well as anyone and I can say for certain that Maxwell Pennington is not working his new ranch without a pretty good-sized crew."

"That's not good."

"Cowboys like to drink and screw and raise hell but they're not all that keen to get into a gunfight. I think we'll be okay . . . but you can stay here in town if you want."

"And miss the chance to see if Emily Pierce is there tied to four bedposts? And to hear what Maxwell has to say about the death and our finding his father buried in the backyard of his father's Virginia City home? Not likely I'll stay here wondering and waiting."

"Fine." Longarm turned abruptly into a gun shop. "You told me earlier that you can shoot straight. I think this is the time to buy you a good gun that you can hide in your dress pocket."

"Do you really think I might need it?"

"I'm pretty damned sure of it."

"Oh, shit," Delia breathed, pasting a smile on her lovely face as they walked up to a counter and saw a row of pistols both used and new for sale.

"What can I help you with today?" the man behind the counter asked.

Longarm turned to Delia. "You have a lot of cash?"

"Enough."

Longarm pivoted back to the gun shop owner. "We'll need a shotgun, a smaller caliber revolver, and a derringer . . . and ammunition."

"My, my!" the man said, beaming with anticipation of

a big profit. "That's quite an order! You must be going to go out and target practice."

"Yeah," Longarm said distractedly as he sized up the arsenal and hoped that they would not have to use it in a short while to defend their lives.

Chapter 21

Longarm was a bit annoyed with the livery in Fallon because the horse that they'd hitched up to the buggy was ancient. It was a thin, sorrel gelding that stumbled constantly in harness and walked at a pace that any desert tortoise could have exceeded.

"Yah!" Longarm growled, snapping the lines across the animal's bony back. "Come on, old fella, we'd like to get to the ranch before sunset."

"Don't hit him," Delia said, placing her hand over Longarm's. "The old guy is doing the best he can."

"You're right," Longarm agreed, feeling guilty about his impatience with the horse that was obviously long past the age of retirement. "But I'll tell you this, Delia, if the shooting starts and we have to make a sudden run for it, we sure as hell don't want to jump into this buggy and try to escape with this horse pulling us."

"I can't really imagine you retreating."

They were on a grade and the sorrel was straining. Longarm pulled on the lines and the gelding stopped, rib cage rapidly expanding and contracting. "Let's give him a moment to catch his breath."

"I'm going to walk to the top of the hill so that will make it a little easier."

"I might as well do the same," Longarm decided. "Besides, I'd like you to test that Colt revolver and derringer. We damn sure want to make sure that they are reliable. And I'll just fire the shotgun a couple times. We need to do that before we come to the ranch gate."

Longarm set the brake though it surely wasn't necessary. The sorrel's head dropped almost to the ground and it stood spraddle-legged sucking wind.

"Here," Longarm said, making sure the Colt and derringer were loaded.

"What should I aim at?"

Longarm studied the ground out ahead of them. "See that juniper. Aim for its trunk."

"It's pretty far. You must think I'm an awfully good shot."

"I don't know what kind of a shot you are," Longarm replied. "But move in close for the derringer and let's see if you can hit the tree from around fifteen or twenty feet."

Longarm stood back. Delia moved toward the tree, the double-barreled derringer in her hand. She raised the little gun, aimed, and fired. Longarm saw wood splinter off the juniper. "Nice shot. Do it again."

Delia fired the derringer a second time and hit the tree squarely.

"Now back up and try the revolver. Here, I'll reload the derringer for you."

"I did pretty good, didn't I," Delia said, looking pleased. "I'd never shot a derringer before."

"You have to get close to make them effective," Longarm said. "But the revolver is accurate for at least fifty feet.

Lift the gun and cock back the hammer. Take a steady aim, then squeeze the trigger."

"I know all that. I have been taught how to shoot before."

"Then let's see you do it."

To Longarm's surprise, Delia didn't hesitate but brought the gun up with both hands, took a moment to aim, and fired. Longarm saw bark splinter off the juniper.

"Not bad. But do it again."

Delia fired twice more, missing once but hitting the tree dead center with her last bullet. "So," she asked, "how about that?"

"Much better than I'd hoped," he admitted. "There are a lot of cowboys who can't shoot that straight."

"I like shooting. Could I try the double-barreled shotgun now?"

"You bought it." He handed the shotgun to Delia. "There's going to be a strong kick so snug it tight against your left shoulder."

"Like this?"

"Exactly. And remember, this is a scattergun and all you have to do is to point it at that juniper and fire."

Delia took a deep breath. "Here goes!"

She pulled *both* triggers and the explosion was so huge that even the sorrel jumped and the juniper shivered as a huge, round patch of its foliage disappeared. Delia staggered backward and would have fallen if Longarm had not caught her in his arms.

"Oh my gawd!" Delia cried. "That was awful!"

"If you think it was awful for you, imagine how our poor juniper must be feeling by now."

Delia shoved the shotgun at Longarm. "You use it and I'll stick to the Colt revolver and two-shot derringer."

"Sounds like a good idea, but it's going to play hell on my already sore shoulder."

"Let's just hope it doesn't come to that," Delia said.

"Amen." Longarm reloaded the shotgun and smiled at the horse. "You finally look like you're awake. We're going to lead you up to the top of this hill just to make things a mite easier."

At the top of the sagebrush-covered hill, they climbed back into the buggy and continued on down the dirt track heading for the Pennington ranch.

"There's the gate!" Longarm exclaimed. "And I can see the house up there in that big stand of cottonwood trees."

"Do we have any kind of a plan?"

"Nope." Longarm squinted into a lowering sun. "Just let me do all the talking."

Delia squeezed his arm. "But I get the strong feeling that you think Emily is being held captive at the Pennington ranch."

"Could be another blond. Let's just not jump to conclusions."

"I understand."

"I just hope she's still alive," Longarm said quietly. "But I'll tell you this much, we're not leaving without finding out one way or the other."

The ranch house was big and made out of lumber as were the barns and what was obviously a bunkhouse with four or five cowboys sitting on its steps talking and smoking cigarettes.

Driving into the yard, Longarm positioned the shotgun across his lap in the direction of the cowboys and said in a low voice, "Delia, put your hand in your dress pocket and your thumb over the hammer of that shooter until we find out if there is going to be a fight."

"I hate to say this," she whispered, "but I'm beginning to think I should have stayed in town."

"And miss all this excitement?" Longarm asked. "Now that sure doesn't seem like your style."

"If we die in a few minutes, my 'style' isn't going to matter."

"We're not going to die," Longarm promised. "If I determine that the game is stacked completely against us, I'll weasel out of this mess and we can come back another time when the odds are more favorable. Trust me, Delia, we didn't come out here to be shot to pieces in a fight we could not win."

"Real glad to hear that."

Longarm painfully raised his left arm and waved at the cowboys as they rolled into the yard. The men had come to their feet and were staring not at him but at Delia, who had a frozen smile on her face. There was no doubt that she was scared and it showed yet it was far too late to change things now.

"Howdy, boys!" Longarm called. "Is Mr. Pennington in the big house?"

A tall and wiry cowboy with a black Stetson and a nice gun and holster stepped out in front of the buggy. Speaking around a twisted cigarette, he drawled, "I'm the ramrod here; what's your business?"

"I need to see Mr. Pennington."

"You didn't answer my question, mister."

"And you didn't answer mine," Longarm retorted as he shifted the shotgun so that it was pointing at the man who had made it clear that he was in charge.

The ramrod swallowed hard and looked over his shoulder at the cowboys who were standing aside and well out of the pattern of the shotgun. Not one of them moved in closer to their ramrod. A few tense moments passed as Longarm and thin man tested each other's wills. Finally, the ramrod tossed his cigarette into the dirt. "I'll go tell Mr. Pennington he's got company."

"Do that," Longarm said without warmth.

The man sauntered up to the house and disappeared inside. Long minutes passed and the cowboys kept staring at Delia. That was fine with Longarm; he'd rather their minds be fixated on sex rather than shooting.

Ten anxious minutes passed before the foreman emerged on the front porch of the ranch house with what had to be Maxwell Pennington right behind. Longarm studied Pennington, noting the man's disheveled appearance. The mine owner now turned rancher's hair was sticking out in all directions and he had not shaved lately. His eyes looked sunken into his face, giving the man a haunted look but even despite all that, he was strikingly handsome as he tucked his wrinkled white shirt into his pants. Longarm also noted that Maxwell Pennington had taken the time to strap a fancy cartridge belt, hand-tooled holster, and a pearl-handled six-gun to his narrow waist.

As the two men left the porch and started toward them, Longarm noted that Maxwell was not walking straight and it occurred to him that the man was either on his way to getting drunk this early in the evening or might have been smoking opium or some other drug.

"Who the hell are you!" Pennington bellowed while still twenty feet away. "I don't know either of you . . . though I'd like to know you better," he said, pointing a finger at Delia.

Longarm heard her whisper, "This doesn't look good."

"No," Longarm whispered back, "it doesn't. Just steady your nerves and be ready for whatever happens next."

Max Pennington halted beside the old gelding's head and so did his grim-faced ramrod, a man that Longarm decided looked more like a professional gunman rather than a working cowboy.

"State your business!" Max demanded.

Longarm had come to a crossroads and knew he could either show Pennington his federal officer's badge or run a game on Pennington. And given that the man's thinking might already be impaired, he decided to run a game.

"Don't you remember us?" he asked, suddenly smiling. "We met in Reno a few months ago in a saloon . . . I forget which . . . but me and my wife here were getting married and you invited us to come on by for a day or two while honeymooning."

The man blinked. "I said that?"

"Why yes," Longarm replied, adding a tone of injury to his voice. "But we were both drinking hard and if you didn't mean it . . ."

"Whoa!" Pennington ran a forearm across his eyes and struggled to gain focus. "If I invited you two to come out here, the least I can do is invite you to come inside and eat and have a drink with me."

"That would be real nice," Delia managed to say. "My husband said you were a gentleman and that you'd be glad to see us."

Pennington shrugged. "Well, sure. What did you say your names were?"

"I'm Custis Long and this is my wife, Delia. We just got hitched in Reno last Saturday."

The foreman turned to his boss. "Mr. Pennington, are you sure about doing this?"

"Yeah, yeah!" Max pivoted around nearly losing his balance. "Grant, have one of the boys unhitch that old horse before it dies where it stands and give it some grain. I could use some company at my supper table."

Grant shook his head. "But . . ."

"Damnit, just do it!"

The tall man's face stiffened but he did as he was ordered. Longarm placed his shotgun down on the floor of the buggy and forced a wide smile directed toward Delia. "See, darlin', I told you he'd be glad to see us."

"Nice place," Delia managed to say.

"I've got some of the finest cattle you'll ever see and the best water rights in the county," Max bragged. "But I got even better imported liquor. Come on inside!"

Longarm took Delia's arm and they moved around the foreman and followed Max into the house. Max shouted, "Hey, Sophia, come meet our guests who are staying for supper!"

Longarm felt Delia's grip on his arm go vise tight a moment before a very thin and pale young woman with blond hair and glassy eyes half stumbled and half shuffled down the staircase in a low-cut, tight-fitting red-lace nightgown. The nightgown was ridiculously short, only barely dropping below the girl's crotch and revealing dark purple bruises on the inside of her thighs. Longarm thought she had the longest and skinniest legs he'd ever seen on a woman.

She looked like a walking cadaver, but it just *had* to be Miss Emily Pierce.

Chapter 22

Delia audibly gasped at the sight of the once beautiful young woman who stood trembling and staring vacantly down at them from the staircase. Emily worked up a weak smile and then lifted her hand and wiggled her fingers in greeting.

"I'm not feeling so well these days," she said, voice small and soft. "But I'm always glad to meet friends of Max. Maybe I'll come down later to see you."

Maxwell Pennington barked a laugh. "Sophia, you need to put on a proper dress, brush your hair and clean up for our guests. I'll have Consuela cook us up something real nice and it'll be good for you to eat."

"You know I can't keep anything down, Max." Her lower lip trembled and her eyes filled with tears. "But . . . but it is so nice of you to come visit."

And then, without another word Emily turned and struggled back up the stairs.

"What's the matter with her?" Delia asked, voice in a stricken voice. "She looks *very* ill."

"She's dying," Max said, blinking and turning away.

"It's a cancer and she's taking some strong medicine for the pain. I don't give her more than another week."

Delia took an involuntary step forward but Longarm caught her hand and stilled her progress, saying, "It's clear that Sophia was once quite beautiful."

"Yes," Max said sadly. "We had planned to get married next June and then she began to feel bad. I took her to a specialist and he finally determined that she has a stomach cancer. I'm just doing the best that I can so she's comfortable but I have to admit that it's breaking my heart."

It took everything Longarm had inside not to grab Maxwell by the throat and throttle the life out of the man, but he needed proof of prior murders. Needed the proof to be able to swear that Maxwell Pennington either was the killer of Marshal John Pierce and his wife, Agnes, or had someone do the killing that day they'd been ambushed and robbed halfway between Reno and Carson. And there was also the murder of the elder Pennington to clear up, although Longarm was pretty sure that the old mine guard, Pete, had been the actual shooter.

"So," Max said, taking Delia's arm and forcing her down the hallway toward his library and bar. "Let's see what we have that you would enjoy in my liquor cabinet. A brandy, perhaps?"

"Whiskey," Delia said in a voice that even Longarm did not recognize.

"Whiskey! You're a woman after my own heart. Tell me, how did I happen not to have seen you in Reno?"

"We haven't been there long."

"Of course." Max turned back to face Longarm. "This is a remarkably beautiful woman. You are indeed a lucky, lucky man."

"I think so."

There was an awkward moment of silence, perhaps

because Maxwell Pennington was waiting to hear more but Longarm would not give him the satisfaction.

"So, Custis, what would you like?"

"I'll also have whiskey."

"That greatly simplifies things because I'll have it as well."

Delia found a place to sit as did Longarm. They watched as Maxwell poured generously and then sloshed the whiskey on his floor delivering their drinks. The man grabbed up his own, raised it, and said, "Here's to your long and happy marriage."

"Thank you," Longarm said as they drank to the toast.

"Well," Max said, throwing his head around and grinning like a circus clown, "what do you do for a living, Custis?"

"I look for things."

"Oh, like what?"

"People, mostly."

"Can I assume you are speaking of *investors*?"

"Maybe."

Delia took another deep swallow of the whiskey and said, "You didn't ask but I'm a dime novelist, Mr. Pennington. Have you read any of my novels under my pen name of Dakota Walker?"

Laughter burst from his mouth. Max took a long drink and wiped tears from his eyes. "Are you serious?"

"I am."

"So you're a dime novelist who calls herself Dakota Walker?"

"That's right." Her voice grew louder and Longarm could hear the building anger. "And I also look for things, only what I look for are stories to tell, and the best ones are murders and kidnappings and all manner of awful acts by—"

"Delia," Longarm interrupted. "Perhaps you need to go upstairs and see if Sophia is all right."

"Ah, she's fine!" Max said with a dismissive wave of his hand.

"I'd feel better," Delia managed to say, "if I just looked in on her for a moment."

"Sophia is probably passed out from the sedation she took just before you arrived. But if she isn't, take her a glass of whiskey. She's grown very fond of the drink since she's been diagnosed with incurable cancer."

Delia came to her feet and refilled her glass, then hurried toward the staircase. Max shouted after her, "Sophia has hallucinations! Wild ones and you just have to tell her that she's . . . she's confused."

"I'll do that," Delia promised, hurrying out of the room.

"So," Max said, turning his attention back to Longarm, "I sure do admire beautiful women and your wife is . . . well, she's stunning."

"Thanks."

"Is she *really* a dime novelist?"

"She really is."

"And I'll bet she writes some pretty bloody prose and then she makes you read it. Am I right?"

"Yep."

Max reached for a cigar box. "Want one?"

"Don't mind if I do."

"Straight from Cuba. The best that money can buy."

They bit off the tips and passed the cigars under their noses. Max grinned proudly and studiously licked his cigar from end to end. He found a match and lit them up.

"So what are you looking for . . . oh, yeah, you said you hunt for people with money to invest."

"I did say that."

"What kind of investment opportunities are you offering?"

Longarm took another sip of his whiskey, looking very

relaxed while his mind was churning. He smiled as if he had a great secret.

"Come on!" Max urged. "I happened to have come into some money recently that I'd like to invest. So, if you have something really special, I insist on hearing about it."

Longarm grinned and took a moment to consider his next words. "Mr. Pennington, I'm afraid that I'd have to take you back to town and show you."

Max leaned back and snorted with derision. "My, aren't you the man of mystery."

"Sorry."

"Does this investment you are handling involve some kind of an invention that has to be seen and not explained?"

"You're sharp, Mr. Pennington. Very sharp."

"Well just try to tell me about it."

"Nope."

The man's eyes hardened. "You're drinking my whiskey and I'm showing you my hospitality, Custis. You sit there in my chair and tell me you can't even give me a hint of what it is that you represent?"

"That's right."

"Damn!" Max surged to his feet and emptied his glass. "I think you are either a fraud or you are toying with my curiosity. Either way, I'm not happy about it and I think this little conversation is about to end."

Longarm also came to his feet. "I regret that you feel that way. However, I have my reasons and if you're not willing to come to Fallon and allow me to show you this amazing invention that I'm offering, that's quite all right."

He set his glass down and walked out of the library. "Delia! Delia, honey, we need to get going."

Delia appeared at the top of stairs, her face pinched with worry. "Sophia is deathly ill. She just had a convulsion and needs to see a doctor at once!"

"I'll come up and help bring her down."

"No!" Max shouted. "She's dying and I don't want her to pass from this world in some small town doctor's back room or in a seedy hotel. She belongs here with me. Right here and I'm not letting her go."

Longarm had been holding it all inside but now his emotions got the better of him and he took three steps forward and drove his fist into Maxwell Pennington's gut. Drove it in so hard and deep that the man actually lifted off the floor and then collapsed, gagging and gulping for air.

"She's *not* your wife," Longarm said, kneeling down beside the gasping man. "And she's deathly ill so I'm taking her to a doctor. If you want to come by tomorrow and check on Sophia and see what I have that will make you a fortune for a modest investment, then please do so."

Maxwell said something unintelligible. Longarm took the stairs at a bound and when he hurried into a bedroom, he saw Sophia stretched out looking more dead than alive. Glancing at Delia, he said, "Grab her a nice dress or two and some clean underwear and let's get her out of here fast!"

Emily weighed almost nothing and Longarm took her quickly down the stairs. Maxwell was heaving on the floor, still unable to get to his feet. Longarm and Delia rushed across the ranch yard and found the buggy and sorrel still hitched.

Longarm lifted Emily up and set her on the seat. Delia jumped up beside her and said, "Here they come!"

Longarm grabbed the double-barreled shotgun and spun around to face Grant and the cowboys. When the cowboys saw him cock back the hammers of the shotgun, they retreated in a hurry, but the ramrod stood his ground.

"Where the hell do you think you're taking her?"

"She's sick. I'm taking her to see a doctor in town."

Grant looked to the house, clearly not sure what he should do next. "Did Mr. Pennington say that was all right?"

"He's not feeling well, either."

"Then I can't let you take her."

Longarm started toward the man, whose face drained of blood. Grant started backpedaling, but Longarm was moving too fast. When he got closer, he brought the butt of the shotgun up and slammed it hard into Grant's pointed, whiskered jaw. The gunman dropped and Longarm kicked him in the ribs, almost certainly cracking a few.

"You cowboys don't want any part of this trouble," he said. "This girl is near death and I'm getting her to a doctor. Try and stop me and I'll blow your guts across that barn wall."

The cowboys shook their heads and making it clear they were not about to provoke a fight and face the devastating blast of two shotgun barrels.

Longarm climbed into the buggy and grabbed up the whip. He laid it down hard on the sorrel's bony back and the buggy lurched forward, slewing around in the dirt and then heading back toward Fallon.

"Holy gawd!" Delia swore, hugging Emily tightly. "How did we do that!"

"We did what we had to do." He glanced sideways at Emily. "Do you think she's going to make it to town?"

"I don't know," Delia choked, brushing strands of Emily's dirty hair from her face. "I'm not a religious person, but right now I'm praying like a preacher."

"Can't hurt," Longarm said, realizing he still had a Cuban cigar clenched between his back teeth. He spit it out and the old sorrel gelding, now heading for its barn, showed surprising vigor.

Chapter 23

"He's coming," Longarm confidently predicted as they stood outside the doctor's office. "Maxwell is consumed by his passions and his greed."

"But you punched him really hard!"

"That's right," Longarm admitted. "The man wasn't going to allow Emily out of his sight so I had no choice. I've seen his type before . . . not often, but often enough to be able to predict that he can't leave me alone until he either settles the score or he is in on what he thinks must be a great invention and opportunity to make money."

"Will Pennington come alone?"

"Not a chance," Longarm told her. "He'll be bringing that gunfighter that poses as a ramrod and everyone else he pays. They'll be heavily armed."

"We need help. What about Sheriff Hopper?"

"I'm going to see him right now. How is Emily doing this morning?"

"She's better and starting to make some sense." Delia shook her head in sadness. "She's been terribly abused."

"Sexually?"

"Yes, sexually and emotionally. I can't even imagine what horrors that monster inflicted."

"Has she said anything about what happened when she and her parents were ambushed?"

"Emily said that a rider wearing a mask rode down and robbed the bodies of her parents after ambushing them from behind a rock. She tried to fight him but he hit her in the face and she passed out. When she came too, Maxwell was kneeling at her side. He told her that he'd chased off the murderer and thief and that he was going to take care of her at his ranch here in Fallon."

"And she believed him?"

"Maxwell had cuts and said he'd had to fight the killer off. He said he'd shot the man as he was riding away and believed the shot was mortal. And he had all her parent's money in the same satchel they'd been carrying to Carson City. It amounted to six thousand dollars."

"He never intended to return her parent's money. And as for the ambusher that he said he shot, nobody in the search parties reported anyone had been shot and killed that day other than Marshal Pierce and his wife."

"Emily doesn't know that. She said that she believed Maxwell was a hero. He took her to the ranch and they drank to the loss of her beloved father and mother."

Longarm nodded with understanding. "And he gave her opium and some powerful drugs and she never really came to her senses. He made her his sex slave."

"Emily says it is all a nightmare and she keeps crying. She is so thin and weak, but you can tell she was very pretty before Maxwell got control and abused her at the ranch."

"What does the doctor say?"

"That she's in terrible shape. Malnutrition. She's been raped and sodomized and . . ."

Delia began to sob, unable to finish.

Longarm took her in his arms and held her tightly. "My guess is that you're not going to put this part of what we're doing into any dime novel."

"Never!"

He kissed the top of her head. "Delia, I like you more and more. You've surprised me in a real good way."

"I'm glad, but what if all those men ride into town tomorrow and gun us down?"

He thought about that for a moment. "Out at the Pennington ranch, we were on their ground and they held all the face cards. Here in town, it's a whole different story. Maxwell Pennington may think he's got the upper hand with all his men but I could tell him that those cowboys aren't going to risk dying for him."

"So now you're going to see Sheriff Hopper?"

"Might as well, although I'm not expecting much."

"He's a coward?"

"No," Longarm said, "but he's not the kind of man to put it all on the line unless he has no other choice."

"He's a disgrace if he won't help us."

"True." Longarm gently pushed Delia away. "Does Emily have anyone in Reno or Carson City to help her recover once this is over in Fallon?"

"Her parents were the only family she knew."

"Then maybe when this trouble passes we ought to take her to Denver. There are specialists there who deal with people who have greatly suffered mentally as well as physically."

"She could come and live with me for awhile," Delia offered, scrubbing away tears. "I have lots of room. It . . . it would be good for me, too."

"I was hoping you might make the offer."

Fifteen minutes later Longarm towered over Sheriff Hopper, who sat slumped behind his desk and said, "I've stated it plainly. You either stand with me, or you get your fat ass out of town never to come back. What's it going to be?"

Hopper was shaking and almost in tears. "Listen, I didn't start any of this and . . ."

"Shut up!" Longarm bellowed. "You're the sheriff and at the doctor's office there's a girl that's been raped, drugged, robbed, and worse. You're either going to stand with me when I make the arrest or you're gone. Which is it to be?"

Hopper scrubbed his sagging chins and then slowly came to his feet. "All right, I'll stand with you. If I leave this town with my tail between my legs, I have nothing and my life is as good as over."

"Get ready for a fight if it comes that."

"Grant Wheeler and Mr. Pennington are both fast with their guns and they hit what they aim for. I'm not all that good with a gun, Marshal Long. I might as well tell you right now that I'm not good at all."

"Then use a shotgun," Longarm ordered. "I'll make the play, but you had damn well better back me if it comes to a showdown."

"I don't have any choice."

"Grab a shotgun and follow me. We're going to go to the hotel and wait for them and that shouldn't be for long."

Hopper grabbed a shotgun, checked to see if it was loaded, then followed Longarm outside. "Oh, gawd, here they come already!"

"Might as well get this over and the sooner the better," Longarm growled. "Just stay back a little and off to one side. If Pennington or his ramrod go for their guns, open fire, but for gawd's sake don't hit me in the back!"

Hopper nodded and licked his lips nervously. He was as white as a ghost and Longarm couldn't miss the tremor in his fingers.

Maxwell Pennington was sitting in a buckboard beside

his ramrod and when they spied Longarm and the sheriff they directed the wagon straight up to them.

"Well, well," Maxwell said, eyes bouncing from Longarm to Hopper and back again. "What's going on here?"

"You're under arrest for the murders of Marshal John Pierce, his wife, Agnes, and your own father. You're going to Reno with me and you'll face a judge and jury, and then you'll sure as hell hang."

Maxwell barked a cold laugh. He looked to his cowboys and then to Grant. "I think that we need to settle this issue promptly, don't you?"

"Yes, sir."

Both men stood up in the buckboard and started to climb down into the street but they didn't quite make it. Sheriff Hopper, scared shitless but seeing no future for himself if he ran, threw the shotgun to his shoulder and screamed, "Gawdamn you, Max! I heard about the little girl over at doc's office! How could you do that to her and her parents?"

"Shut the fuck up," Grant hissed.

"*You* shut the fuck up!" Hopper cried an instant before he pulled the trigger.

The gunfighter didn't have a chance. Grant Wheeler's long, thin body was hurled backward by the blast. Maxwell hesitated for a mere split second, then swore and went for his gun. Longarm's gun was already coming out of his holster. Maxwell was faster on the draw, but he'd gotten a late start and Longarm shot him right through the heart twice just for good measure and pure satisfaction.

Two of the Pennington ranch cowboys threw themselves off their ponies and went racing down the street on foot, yelling bloody murder. The others spurred their horses into a hard run out of town. The fine Pennington buggy horse danced in fear, nostrils flaring at the scent and sight of so much blood.

Longarm turned to Sheriff Hopper, who was shaking badly. "You kind of jumped the gun, didn't you?"

"I . . . I guess."

"Well," Longarm said, staring at the two dead men, "I suppose this pretty much guarantees you'll get reelected."

Hopper's head bobbed up and down and the shotgun slipped unnoticed from his chubby hands. He couldn't tear his eyes off what he'd done to the gunfighter. "I guess they will reelect me," he finally managed to say.

Longarm clapped the fat lawman on the shoulder. "You probably ought to go into the nearest saloon and get a bottle."

"Yeah. Good idea." Hopper finally managed to look at Longarm. "What about you?"

"I'm going to the bank here and drawing six thousand out of Pennington's account . . . the money that he stole from her parents. After that we're leaving with Emily and won't ever be back."

"Thank gawd."

Longarm smiled and holstered his gun. He saw Delia burst out of the hotel and come running toward him, arms spread wide.

"Everything is going to be just fine," he said to Hopper and himself as he went to meet his beautiful dime novelist.

GIANT-SIZED ADVENTURE FROM AVENGING ANGEL LONGARM.

BY TABOR EVANS

penguin.com/actionwesterns

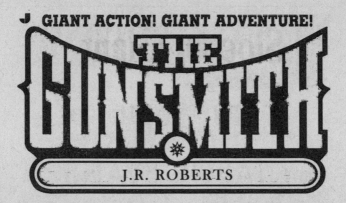

GIANT ACTION! GIANT ADVENTURE!

THE GUNSMITH

J.R. ROBERTS

penguin.com/actionwesterns

M455AS0812

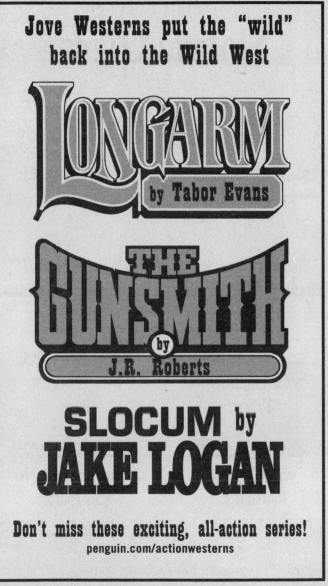

DON'T MISS A YEAR OF

Slocum Giant
by
Jake Logan

Slocum Giant 2004:
Slocum in the Secret
Service

Slocum Giant 2005:
Slocum and the Larcenous
Lady

Slocum Giant 2006:
Slocum and the Hanging
Horse

Slocum Giant 2007:
Slocum and the Celestial
Bones

Slocum Giant 2008:
Slocum and the Town
Killers

Slocum Giant 2009:
Slocum's Great
Race

Slocum Giant 2010:
Slocum Along
Rotten Row

Slocum Giant 2013:
Slocum and the Silver
City Harlot

penguin.com/actionwesterns

M457AS0812